W9-AZX-518

No Way Out

Peggy Kern

Series Editor: Paul Langan

TOWNSEND PRESS
www.townsendpress.com

Books in the Bluford Series

Copyright © 2009 by Townsend Press, Inc.
Printed in the United States of America

9 8 7 6 5

Cover illustration © 2009 by Gerald Purnell

Townsend Press, Inc.
439 Kelley Drive
West Berlin, NJ 08091
cs@townsendpress.com

ISBN-13: 978-1-59194-176-**7**
ISBN-10: 1-59194-176-8

Library of Congress Control Number:
2008907030

Chapter 1

Harold Davis took a deep breath and slowly started to peel the gauze from the wound on his grandmother's leg.

"Hold on, Grandma. I'm almost done," he said quietly.

"Don't worry, baby. It doesn't hurt too much," she replied, wincing slightly. "Just take your time."

Harold glanced up at his grandmother lying on the couch. He could tell she was in pain from the way she gripped the cushions, but still she managed to smile back at him.

"Go ahead, child. Really, it's okay," she insisted.

Harold gently peeled away the sticky gauze and looked at the large, swollen wound. It was blood red, with a white film along the edges.

It looks angry, Harold thought as he

1

carefully spread ointment over the cut and covered it with a clean bandage. He hated looking at her leg, but he knew he had no choice. It was her first day out of the hospital, and she needed his help.

"Okay Grandma, all done. I'll get dinner started," Harold said as he turned the television to her favorite channel and put away her medical supplies. "Those bandages the hospital gave us are cheap. We need the more expensive kind that won't stick so much. Like the doctor said."

"Oh Harold," Grandma sighed, struggling to sit up on the couch. "I'm sorry you have to do all this for me. But don't you worry. Just a few more weeks, and I'll be good as new." She smoothed out her long floral housedress and fussed with her hair as she talked. "Just as good as new."

"I know, Grandma," he said, forcing himself not to stare at the deep purple bruise that covered the left side of her forehead. He wanted her words to be true, but after the events of the last few days, he wasn't sure. Grandma had turned seventy-three last month, and today she seemed even older.

At least she's home again, he thought

2

to himself. *At least we're home.*

Two days ago, Grandma fell on the front steps of their apartment building, banging her head on the pavement, spraining her ankle, and cutting her leg badly. Mr. Harris, their neighbor, had found her lying on the sidewalk and called an ambulance. He'd also driven to Bluford High, where Harold was a freshman, to take him to the hospital. Harold shuddered as the events of that day flashed in his mind like a nightmare.

He had been in the middle of Ms. Webb's algebra class when Ms. Spencer, the school principal, rushed into his classroom.

"Harold, I need you in the office," she said, her voice tense. "*Now.*"

Everyone in the class turned to face him.

"Boy, don't tell me *you're* in trouble. You don't do nothin' wrong," said Rodney Banks.

"Maybe he broke into the cafeteria. Look at his stomach. You *know* that boy likes to eat," added Andre Jenkins with a smirk. Harold cringed in embarrassment.

"Man, leave him alone," snapped Darrell Mercer, Harold's friend. "This ain't any of your business."

"That's enough, gentlemen!" warned Ms. Webb as Harold left the classroom.

When Harold arrived at the principal's office, Mr. Harris was standing at the counter, quietly arguing with Ms. Bader, the school secretary.

Why's he here? Harold wondered.

Mr. Harris lived in the small apartment at the end of their hallway. He'd moved in a few months ago, though in that time, Harold had hardly said a word to him.

"I'm sorry, but you're not on the list, Mr. Harris. We cannot let you drive Harold to the hospital," Ms. Bader explained.

Mr. Harris's eyes were focused and determined. "I understand," he replied calmly. "But his grandmother asked me to come. She doesn't want him to be scared."

"I'm sure that's true, but I can't change school policy, Mr. Harris—"

"What happened?" Harold asked, interrupting them. "What happened to Grandma?"

The office suddenly grew silent. Harold saw the concern on Ms. Bader's face, but before she could reply, Mr. Harris stepped forward, putting his hand on Harold's shoulder. A thin streak of dried blood stained his sleeve. Harold's heart raced.

"It's all right. She's all right," Mr. Harris said calmly. "She fell down and banged herself up pretty bad, but I've seen worse. She's at the hospital now. Your teachers are going to take you over there right now," he said, glancing back at Ms. Bader and Ms. Spencer. "I'll be right behind you."

At the hospital, Harold sat for hours beneath the buzzing fluorescent lights of the crowded waiting room. Doctors hurried back and forth. Families wandered in and out, some in tears. He needed to use the bathroom, but he didn't want to get up in case the doctors came looking for him.

Finally, well after sunset, a doctor sat next to him and described what happened. Harold felt dizzy when the doctor began explaining the details of Grandma's condition.

Significant leg abrasion and minor head trauma.

Diabetes, obesity, and age complicate her injuries.

Slow recovery. Constant care may be required.

Harold stared at the floor, his head

throbbing at the news. After the doctor left, he was visited by a social worker, a young woman with neat hair and lipstick and shoes that clicked on the floor as she walked. She asked Harold questions that haunted him ever since.

"Do you have any other family, Harold? Is there someone you can stay with?"

She paused, waiting for him to answer. Harold stared at the dirty flecks in the tile floor.

"If not, we'll need to place you somewhere while your grandmother—"

"No! I'm staying *here!*" he insisted, jumping out of his chair and backing away from her like an animal about to be trapped. "I'm staying with Grandma." He knew he sounded like a child, but he couldn't help it.

He was shaking with panic, his heart pounding frantically as the full meaning of her words sank in. *There was no other family.* His mom died in childbirth with him, and his father had run out shortly after that. He had no one else to stay with. His eyes burned with tears, and he looked around desperately. He thought he might throw up, right there on the hospital floor.

Just then, Mr. Harris stepped forward. Had he been there the entire time? Harold couldn't recall. The evening had been a blur.

"The boy can stay with me tonight, ma'am," Mr. Harris said quietly. "I live just up the hall from his apartment. I'm sure Mrs. Davis will give her consent."

Harold stayed at Mr. Harris's that evening and the next, sleeping on a fold-out sofa at night and visiting Grandma at the hospital all day. Though just two days passed since Grandma fell, their apartment felt like a foreign place to Harold when they returned.

Normally it was filled with the aroma of his grandmother's cooking. But when Harold unlocked the door and helped Grandma in, it smelled stale and musty. He knew he'd need to clean it, but first he had to cook dinner.

Harold poked around the fridge. The milk was already starting to sour. There weren't enough eggs for tomorrow's breakfast. Fortunately, Mr. Harris had dropped off a tray of lasagna. Harold took it out of the refrigerator and put it in the stove, turning it to 350 degrees as Mr. Harris said. Then he returned to the living room to check on Grandma.

The usually clean living room was now cluttered with bandages, unanswered mail and the bulky wooden crutches from the hospital. Pillows were piled awkwardly on the couch to keep Grandma's ankle elevated. A bag of dirty laundry sat in the corner where she left it two days ago, still waiting to be washed.

"My goodness, this place is a mess," Grandma said, almost to herself. "Now, don't you worry about all this, Harold. I just need to rest up for a little while and we'll be back to our normal schedule. Don't you forget about your homework, either," she added. "I might need to stay off this leg for a few weeks, but that don't mean I won't be checking on you."

"Yes, Grandma," he replied, rubbing his temples. He could feel a dull headache starting to build behind his eyes.

School's the least of my worries now, Grandma, he wanted to say. Dishes needed to be washed. Laundry needed to be done. The bathroom needed scrubbing. Groceries needed to be bought. And more than anything, Grandma needed his help.

"Do you have any other family, Harold? Is there someone you can stay

with?" The social worker's questions echoed in his mind again. Harold shuddered, his headache worsening.

Harold rummaged through the cabinets for some clean dinner plates. Unless he was hungry, he rarely came into the kitchen. He spent most of his time in the living room watching television or doing his homework at their small table. The kitchen was Grandma's territory, and Harold felt lost among the pots and pans and plastic containers of flour, spices, and odd foods he could not identify. There were shelves of canned peaches and sweet potatoes, which she would use to make pies.

Was she still allowed to eat pie? he wondered.

The hospital had sent them home with a list of "approved" foods for his grandmother, but he hadn't had a chance to read the list yet. Harold didn't really understand her diabetes. She'd had the disease for a long time and it never seemed to be a problem before. But at the hospital, her doctors discovered some sores on her feet when they examined her. They said she could have "complications" if she didn't control her weight and diet.

9

Harold found the dinner plates piled in the sink. He washed two plates and checked on Mr. Harris's lasagna. After five minutes in the oven, it was still cool, especially in the middle.

"Grandma," he called, turning up the oven dial to 400 degrees. "How long does it take to heat up lasagna?"

There was no reply.

"Grandma?" he repeated, waiting for a response that didn't come. "*Grandma?*"

He rushed into the living room, his heart suddenly pounding. His grandmother lay still, asleep on the couch. Her head leaned to one side, and her chest rose and fell heavily with each breath. He could see the swollen bruise on her forehead and the bandage peeking out from beneath her long dress. It was already turning brown, even though he just changed the dressing. He turned off the television and covered her with a blanket—what she usually did for him when he was sick.

"How are we gonna get through this, Grandma?" he whispered as he leaned over her, gently kissing her forehead. "Who's gonna make dinner while your leg heals?" Harold swallowed hard, and stood up.

What if it doesn't? he wondered.

Harold's head throbbed now. He was hungry and exhausted, and he didn't want to think any more. He ate a piece of Mr. Harris's lukewarm lasagna and washed the dishes. Then he grabbed a pillow and blanket from his bedroom and sat on the floor by the couch.

The apartment was silent, except for his grandmother's breathing and the occasional siren outside.

"Do you have any other family, Harold? Is there someone you can stay with?"

In the dark apartment, the questions crashed down on him in endless waves.

"There's no one else," he whispered into the darkness. "We're alone."

Chapter 2

The next morning, Grandma sat for a long time at the kitchen table, sifting through the mound of paperwork from the hospital. Her leg was propped up on a chair, and her forehead was wrinkled with worry.

"My Lord, these insurance companies will be the death of me!" she suddenly exclaimed.

Harold cringed at her words. "What's wrong?"

Grandma looked up in surprise, as if she'd forgotten he was there.

"I'm sorry, Harold. It's just . . ."

She hesitated for a moment and looked at him thoughtfully.

"Come sit down, child. We need to talk."

Harold sat across from his grandmother and studied her face: the deep creases around her mouth, the gray hair that grew in patches on her head, the dark, heavy bags under her eyes. The strong woman who'd kept watch over him all his life now seemed weary and weak. Vulnerable. He looked away, afraid she could read his thoughts.

"We're gonna need to be real careful with money for a while. Real careful," Grandma said, reaching across the table and grabbing hold of Harold's hand. "I hate to worry you, child. But you'll be doing the shopping till I get back on my feet, and I need you to mind our budget." As she talked, she gazed at the faded picture of her husband, Harold's deceased grandfather, which hung over the front door.

"Besides," she added with a sigh. "You're fifteen now. I suppose it's time I started teaching you about these things. Lord knows I'm not gettin' any younger."

Harold fidgeted in his chair, still unable to look into her face. He hated what she was saying but knew it was true.

"Are we gonna be okay?" Harold asked, his eyes fixed on the old photograph of his dead grandfather.

Grandma squeezed his hand. "Of course we are, child. I've been around for a lot of years. I've seen many hard times in my life. This time ain't no worse than the others. I can make a dollar last a week if I have to. And once this leg heals, maybe I can start selling my cakes like I used to when you were a little boy. Or I can do laundry for the neighbors."

Harold cringed at the thought of Grandma doing other people's laundry. He knew how hard it was for her to keep up with their housework. There was no way she could handle more, especially not with her medical condition.

"Maybe *I* should get a job," he suggested.

"You *got* a job, Harold. Your job is to keep your grades up and get your education," declared Grandma in a firm voice. "I know you want to help, but I don't want you neglecting your schoolwork over some job that don't pay more than what it costs to take the bus there. And I won't have you wandering this neighborhood at night, either. No, Harold, you worry about school. I'll worry about how we gonna pay for what we need."

Grandma sighed and slumped back in her chair as if their talk drained her. "Lord, I'm just so *tired*," she said, touching the bruise on her head.

"Maybe you should lay down," said Harold. "Don't you gotta do that blood test, too?" Along with her new diet, Grandma needed to test her blood sugar level every few hours. The doctor at the hospital reviewed this with them before sending Grandma home.

"Is it time already?" she asked as Harold helped her to the couch and handed her the small blue kit that said *Glucometer* across the side.

"All these instructions and lists and medications," she added. "My goodness."

Harold returned to the kitchen. He didn't like watching his grandmother poke her finger for the blood test. As he passed the table, he noticed the stack of papers Grandma had been working on. He paused, curious about what she read that got her so upset. He knew he shouldn't look at her mail.

But she looked so worried, he thought. He quickly scanned the top sheet. It was a bill from the emergency room. The words at the bottom of the page jumped out at him.

Total Amount Due: $837.83

Harold flushed and glanced back at Grandma. She jabbed the tip of her finger

15

with a short needle. A dark pearl of blood dripped onto the white tab she was holding.

Harold turned so his back blocked her view of what he was doing. Then he flipped to the next letter. It was another bill, this time for the hospital room. His eyes raced to the bottom line.

Total Amount Due: $2,454.17

Harold's pulse began to throb. He turned quickly to the next item, a tan envelope with an official-looking seal that read, "Department of Family Services." In the center, in bold black ink, were the words: "Regarding Harold Davis." He picked up the envelope.

"*Harold,*" Grandma called from behind him, shattering his thoughts. He dropped the papers and quickly stepped away from the table.

"I need you to go to the store," she continued. "And bring me all that paper-work on the table. I don't want you snooping around. That's *my* business, y'hear?"

"Yes, Grandma," he said, gathering the stack and bringing it to her. He was relieved to see she was distracted with her test kit. She didn't seem to notice that he'd read anything.

Still, Harold wondered about that envelope. What was inside it?

Just then, there was a knock at the door. Harold looked through the eyehole to see Cindy Gibson, his neighbor and classmate. A familiar nervous twinge raced to the pit of his stomach.

"Hey, Harold," she said softly as he opened the door. She was wearing a tight-fitting tank top and baggy sweat-pants, and her dark hair was pulled back into a ponytail. She was carrying a small bundle of flowers.

"Hi Cindy," Harold answered, glancing at her amber eyes and cinnamon skin. He suddenly felt awkward in his T-shirt, wet from washing dishes.

Since eighth grade, he'd liked Cindy, though he never told her how he felt, not exactly. There was no point, he figured. He learned that months ago when he asked her to the movies. At the time, she was seeing Bobby Wallace, a Bluford senior who messed with drugs and hit his girlfriends, including Cindy. Harold hated him.

"You're really nice . . . but me and Bobby are together," she'd said. *"Can't you just be my friend and be happy for me?"*

Her words were devastating. It had taken him weeks to build up the courage to ask her out. And yet he wasn't surprised at her reaction. Girls usually ignored him. Those who didn't often joined other Bluford students in teasing him about his weight.

"Someone get that boy a bra."

"He so fat he has his own zip code."

"Dude needs a driveway to iron his shirt."

He'd heard the jokes since middle school. Cindy would never go out with someone like him. Harold was sure of it. He accepted that they'd just be friends, but he still couldn't stop his palms from sweating whenever she was around, even now.

"What's up?" he asked.

"Mr. Harris told me about your grandmother," Cindy said. "Is she okay?" Harold could hear the worry in Cindy's voice.

"Yeah, she's gettin' better," he said, trying to sound confident. He knew Cindy loved his grandmother. They had grown close a few months ago when Cindy was having trouble at home with her mom. Grandma knew Cindy needed someone to talk to, so she started inviting her over.

For a while, it seemed to Harold that

Grandma had two grandkids—him and Cindy. He didn't mind. It was nice to watch TV with Cindy or see her smile when she tasted Grandma's sweet potato pie. But lately she'd been visiting less. Harold figured she and her mother were getting along again.

"Harold?" Grandma's voice snapped him from his thoughts. "Is that my Cindy at the door?"

Cindy smiled. To Harold, the entire hallway suddenly seemed brighter.

"I think someone wants to see you," he said, grinning back at her.

Cindy walked in and froze for a half second at the sight of Grandma. Harold thought he heard a slight gasp as Cindy glanced at the large bruise the color of eggplant on Grandma's forehead.

"Grandma Rose!" she said, leaning down to give Grandma a hug. "I'm so glad you're home."

Grandma winced as Cindy embraced her. "Ooh, honey, be gentle now. I'm sore all over."

"Sorry!" Cindy cried, letting Grandma go. "I was just so scared."

Harold noticed tears in Cindy's eyes. He'd already grown used to the sight of Grandma's injuries, but Cindy was seeing them for the first time. For some reason, her reaction made him want to cry too, and he had to look away.

"Sit down, child," Grandma said to her. "Don't you worry. I'm gonna be just fine, just fine. Last thing I want is you gettin' all upset over me. Bad enough havin' Harold fussin' over me all the time."

"Okay," Cindy said, nodding and wiping her eyes. "I brought these for you. They're from me and my mom." She handed the bunched flowers to Grandma.

"Why thank you, honeychild! It's been a long time since someone got me flowers," Grandma replied with a tired laugh.

"I also have your algebra homework from Friday, Harold," Cindy added, turning to him.

"Thanks," Harold replied, wishing she could take it back.

"You're a good girl, child," Grandma said, patting Cindy's face lovingly. "I told that boy he should've gone to school, but he insisted on staying with me at the hospital. I'm just so grateful to Mr. Harris for looking after Harold. I swear this neighborhood could use more men like him. He was in the Marines, you know. Just like my husband, rest his soul." Grandma glanced at the photograph on

20

the wall again. "Of course, my husband fought in the Korean War, you know."

"Grandma," Harold groaned. "You've told her this story a million times already."

"Okay, okay," Grandma replied, waving her hand good-naturedly. "Cindy, maybe you could go to SuperFoods with Harold," she suggested. "I need him to pick up groceries."

"Grandma," Harold protested. "Maybe she has other things to do today."

"No, I can go," Cindy offered, her voice sincere.

"Now remember what we talked about, Harold," said Grandma as she handed him a grocery list and a small roll of cash. "Stick to this list. Nothing extra—no chips, no cookies, no soda. We need to mind our budget. And don't you talk to those James brothers neither. Those boys been hanging around the supermarket again, and I just *know* they're up to no good. Straight home, y'hear?"

"Yes, Grandma," Harold grumbled.

* * *

Harold and Cindy walked down the sidewalk, between the dull concrete apartment buildings that lined their street. It was a hot spring day—sunny and sticky, with a breeze that barely stirred the sweaty air. Still, Harold was glad to get away from the cluttered apartment and the pressure of caring for his grandmother.

He was also glad to be with Cindy.

"Thanks for coming over," Harold said. "It meant a lot to Grandma." He wanted to tell her it meant a lot to him too, but he couldn't bring himself to say the words.

"I just can't believe what happened," Cindy said, shaking her head. "I mean that bruise."

"You should see her leg," he replied, shuddering at the thought of changing her bandage later. "And her ankle, and the sores on her feet."

"Harold," Cindy said, glancing up at the empty third floor apartment window where Grandma usually sat watching over their neighborhood like a mother hawk. "Are you gonna be okay with everything?"

He could feel her staring at him, but he kept his eyes on the sidewalk.

"I have to be," he said, unable to lie. "I mean, what choice do I have?"

A bus rumbled loudly up the block then. Harold was grateful for the interruption. Without a word, they crossed the street to SuperFoods.

"Oh, great," Cindy fumed with a disgusted look on her face. "Look who's back."

Harold looked up to see Londell James standing outside of SuperFoods, smoking a cigarette and talking with a group of younger boys. Londell was tall and muscular, with a sharp, angular face and thin lips. He towered over the other boys who gathered around him like students in a class.

"I thought he was in jail," Harold said, suddenly feeling nervous. Everyone at Bluford knew Londell. He was involved in a shooting last year. Roylin Bailey, a junior at Bluford, had been grazed by the bullet. Harold wasn't there, but his grandma told him how the shots were fired in broad daylight near a park not far from the high school.

I hate to say this about anyone's child, but it'll be a good day for this neighborhood when Londell James is put in jail," Grandma said at the time.

"He *was* in jail," Cindy replied. "But Roylin's sister told me they let him out 'cause no one could prove he did any-thing except drive his car that day. No witnesses came forward. People were too scared."

"That's messed up," Harold replied, wondering if he should turn around and go home. He'd gone to middle school with Londell's younger brother, Jupiter, who was also standing outside. When they were in school, Jupiter's mom spent time in jail for selling drugs out of her home. Jupiter's father had been stabbed to death in a fight at a bar when they were in seventh grade.

"Those poor boys never got to be chil-dren," Grandma told him when she heard the news. He never forgot the sad look on her face. Harold hadn't seen Jupiter since seventh grade. Last he heard, Jupiter was in a foster home on the other side of town.

"Maybe we should come back when they're not here," Cindy whispered.

Harold felt the same way, but he knew he needed to shop for Grandma. "I can't. We need groceries now," he said.

Cindy grabbed Harold's arm as they approached the supermarket. He could tell she was scared by the way she held onto him; Harold was scared, too, but he did his best to look calm and confident. The boys stopped talking as they approached. Harold noticed Jupiter watching them.

"Yo, check out this fat boy," said a tall, thin boy Harold didn't recognize. He was wearing a basketball jersey. A younger boy stood next to him, carrying a bright yellow backpack. He didn't look more than ten years old.

"I know you," said Jupiter with a smirk.

"'Sup, Jupiter," said Harold, trying his best to sound casual.

"Yeah. I remember you from middle school. You was fat back then, too."

The boys laughed and nudged each other approvingly.

"Yeah, he fat! Like a sausage or somethin'," shouted the tall boy.

"Yo, where's your grandma? She used to take you everywhere back in the day. I bet she still changes your diapers," Jupiter barked.

Harold's face burned with embarrassment. He wanted to say something to shut them up, but he knew that could make things worse.

"Just ignore them, Harold," whispered Cindy. "We don't want any trouble."

"Ain't that sweet. His girlfriend protectin' him," Jupiter continued.

Great, Harold thought. *Now she's really gonna think I'm a loser.*

Londell watched Harold through a gray cloud of cigarette smoke. "Joop, step off him!" he snapped angrily. "What I tell y'all about actin' like kids?"

His voice had an immediate effect. Jupiter and the rest of the boys shrank back, their eyes lowered as if they were scared.

Londell nodded at Harold, as if to say that it was safe for him to pass. Harold nodded back and quickly made his way into the supermarket, relieved that Londell had intervened.

Thirty minutes later, Harold and Cindy unloaded their groceries at the checkout counter.

"I'm so glad we found these bandages!" Harold exclaimed, examining the box of gauze as if it was a treasure. "These don't stick so much, and Grandma can leave 'em on for the whole day. The doctor said her leg will heal much faster with these."

For the first time since Grandma's fall, Harold felt a glimmer of hope. Maybe with the bandages it wouldn't be too long before she was back on her feet, and everything would be back to normal.

"Thanks for coming with me, Cindy," said Harold. "It's really nice to have you around."

Cindy smiled and looked at the floor. Harold thought about how she'd grabbed him before, like he could actually protect her. He felt proud with Cindy on his arm, and he liked that she hadn't let go, even when Jupiter had called her his girlfriend. Harold moved closer to her, their hands almost touching.

"Your total is $83.13," said the cashier.

Harold took out the wad of cash and began counting. He had seventy dollars.

He looked up at the cashier, then at Cindy, and the line of customers behind them. A wave of shame rushed over his face.

"Uh, I don't have—"

"Is there a problem?" the cashier asked impatiently.

"What's wrong?" asked Cindy.

"*Nothing!*" Harold snapped. "I mean . . ."

He tried to think of some excuse he could tell the cashier. He searched his pockets, although he knew they were empty. "It's just, I'm a little short.

27

Thirteen dollars short."

The cashier sighed and rolled her eyes. "Well then, you'll have to put something back."

Harold looked at the groceries. There was nothing extra, only what Grandma had put on the list.

"But we need everything," he said desperately. "What about the apples? Can I leave those?"

"They only cost two dollars," said the cashier. "What about these?" She picked up the box of bandages. "They cost $16.50."

"*No!*" Harold yelled, yanking them from her hand. "I need those!"

"C'mon, kid. We ain't got all day," barked the man behind them in line.

The cashier picked up a phone and pressed a red button. "I need a manager at checkout please!" Her voice boomed through the entire store.

"Wait!" begged Harold. "I-I just need to think for a minute."

"Harold, maybe we should leave the bandages. We can always come back later for them," Cindy suggested.

"No! We can't!" he snapped, embarrassed that Cindy was seeing this. "You don't understand! My grandmother *needs* these." Harold shook his head and stared at the floor. His shoulders sank in defeat.

"Sorry, kid. I know how it is. But this ain't a charity. I need you to pay, or move on. I have other customers to deal with," said the cashier.

"Lady, *please*," groaned Harold. "You don't understand."

"I got it," said a deep voice. Harold turned to see Londell James pulling out a thick roll of cash from his leather jacket. "How much does he owe?"

The cashier looked at Harold. "$13.13," she grumbled.

Londell handed a twenty dollar bill to the cashier. "Gimme a pack of smokes, too. And a candy bar for the little man here."

"We don't need your money," snapped Cindy. "Ain't that right, Harold?"

Harold shrugged. His heart was pounding, and his forehead was beaded with sweat. "I need those bandages, Cindy."

"Harold," she insisted. "*I'll* give you the money. I'll have it after I babysit this weekend."

Harold felt humiliated. He didn't want to be Cindy's charity case. And he didn't want Londell's money, but he was desperate. He had to do something for Grandma. *Now.*

Londell eyed them intently.

"We need these bandages today, Cindy. Thanks, but I can't wait," he whispered back.

Cindy shook her head, as if he'd just insulted her. "Grandma Rose wouldn't want you taking money from *him.* You know that."

"But Cindy—"

"Whatever, Harold," she snapped, her voice a mixture of anger and frustration. "Do what you want. I'll see you later." Cindy brushed past Londell and out the door.

Londell smiled at Harold and picked up several bags of groceries. "Sorry about what my brother said before. Those boys need to learn some self-control," he said.

"My groceries," said Harold, eyeing the bags in Londell's hands. "I need them."

Londell laughed. "What, you think I'm gonna steal them? C'mon. I'll walk you home. Consider it an apology for what happened outside."

Harold shrugged, unsure of what to say or do. Londell didn't seem like someone he needed to be afraid of. "Okay, I guess," he said.

Londell and Harold walked down the street toward Harold's block. They passed Londell's boys again, only this time they were silent as Harold walked by.

"Thanks for the money. My Grandma . . . she's sick. Otherwise I wouldn't have—"

"Taken money from me?" Londell said with a knowing smile. "Guess you've heard about me, huh?"

You shot Roylin, Harold thought to himself. *You were in jail.*

"I made some mistakes last year. Big mistakes, but that's ancient history," said Londell, as if he could read Harold's mind. "I got it all figured out now. In my line of work, you can't draw attention to yourself like that. I know that now."

Harold knew what kind of "work" Londell was talking about: *Drugs.*

All Harold's life, Grandma had warned him about the guys on the corner at all hours. Londell had been one of them. There wasn't a day that went by where Grandma wasn't telling him to come straight home and stay away from guys like Londell. He knew Grandma would be furious if she found out he'd taken Londell's money.

31

But what choice did I have, he thought.

"You got parents at home?" Londell asked.

Harold shook his head. "Nah."

Londell nodded. "It's not easy, raising yourself."

"I got my grandma," Harold said defensively.

"Yeah, but you said she's sick, right? A man's got to think about the future. You know, in case something happens. Trust me, I know."

Harold stopped at the corner before his apartment building. "I can take it from here," he said.

"Don't want Grandma to see you walking with me, huh?"

Harold smiled despite himself. "Yeah. She wouldn't like that."

Londell studied Harold for a moment. "Don't believe everything you hear. I ain't that bad. I helped *you* out, right?" Londell carefully placed the groceries on the sidewalk. "Remember that."

"Thanks again for the money," said Harold. "I'll pay you back. I swear."

Londell smiled and shook Harold's hand. "Don't worry about it. Maybe someday I'll need a favor and you can help me out. Like I said, men like us got to think about the future. We ain't got parents to take care of things." Londell put his hand on Harold's shoulder. "But you know that, don't you?"

I do, thought Harold as he picked up the groceries, glancing back to watch Londell stride confidently down the street, as if he didn't have a care in the world.

Chapter 3

"Hey, fat boy's back! What up, fat boy?"

Harold barely made it through the doorway of Mr. Mitchell's classroom Monday morning before Rodney Banks started up.

"Shut up, Rodney," yelled Darrell Mercer from the back of the room. "Nobody wants to hear your mouth."

Harold kept his head down and walked to his desk in the back row. He passed Cindy, but she didn't look up. Harold could feel the class staring at him. He knew everyone was wondering why Ms. Spencer sent him to the office last week.

"What's up, bro?" asked Darrell with a smile.

Harold nodded and dropped his backpack on the floor, slumping wearily into his seat. He was glad to see Darrell, but he was also tired. He'd gotten up an hour early to help Grandma with breakfast and barely made it to school on time.

"You okay?" asked Darrell. "Cindy told me your grandma got hurt."

"Yeah," Harold answered with a shrug. "She fell, but she's all right," he said, thinking of the stained bandage he'd changed this morning. He didn't feel like talking about Grandma or anything else from the past few days.

"Yo, Harold, I heard the cafeteria ladies missed you," Rodney teased from across the classroom. "They were mad 'cause you weren't there to suck up the extra food." Rodney made a sucking sound, and a number of students burst into laughter.

Harold squirmed in his seat and glanced at Cindy. She sat at her desk and scribbled in her notebook, not once looking back at him.

Great. She's ignoring me, Harold thought. *First the grocery store, and now this.*

"Rodney, your mouth's so big, they coulda shoved all the extra food in it and you *still* wouldn't shut up," cut in Darrell. Hoots erupted at Darrell's comment. Rodney stood up at his desk.

"What's the matter, Darrell? Your fat girlfriend need you to stick up for her?"

Harold cringed. Sweat gathered under his arms as the class roared even louder. He felt everyone's eyes on him.

"That's enough!" boomed a familiar voice. Harold turned to see Mr. Mitchell walk into class. "Sit down, Rodney. The next person to speak is headed to Ms. Spencer's office. Understood?"

"I got your back, man. Don't worry," Darrell whispered.

Harold nodded weakly. He was glad Darrell was there. But Harold was also ashamed that he needed his friend to stick up for him. He wished he could be like Londell James, a person who could make everyone shut up with a single word.

The class quieted down, though Rodney shot Harold a menacing glare before turning around in his seat.

"Welcome back, Harold," said Mr. Mitchell with a smile.

"Thanks," Harold mumbled. *Great to be here*, he thought bitterly.

* * *

At lunchtime, Harold stood at the back of the cafeteria and looked around the room miserably. He hated lunch period. Most days he sat with Darrell, but he didn't see him at their usual table.

Harold glanced over at Cindy's table. She was sitting nearby with Amberlynn and several other girls who were chatting and laughing together.

"Girl, what's *wrong* with you today?" he overheard Amberlynn say. "You're so quiet!"

Then he saw Darrell waving.

"Yo, Harold! Come sit with us," he shouted. Harold looked over and groaned. The table was full of Darrell's friends from the wrestling team. Harold always felt awkward around them. Darrell once felt the same way, but that changed when he joined the team. Sometimes Harold wondered why Darrell was still his friend.

"C'mon man, hurry up! Let's eat!" Darrell yelled.

Harold forced himself to walk over and join them. "What's up?" he said quietly, to no one in particular. The table was crowded with trays of spaghetti and meatballs, and the boys were busy shoveling down forkloads. Only one of them looked up at Harold.

"'Sup," he grunted between bites.

Darrell laughed. "Don't mind them. They're just hungry. Where's your lunch?"

"It's in my bag." Harold fumbled with his backpack and pulled out a flattened peanut butter and jelly sandwich.

Darrell looked surprised. "I *know* you ain't missin' spaghetti day. It's your favorite."

"It is. I just . . . was late this morning and forgot to grab money on my way out." Harold felt guilty for lying, but he didn't want to tell Darrell the truth. After breakfast, Grandma had fallen into a deep sleep on the couch. He didn't have the heart to wake her up and ask her for money, especially since he knew how tight things were. Instead, he threw together a sandwich and raced out the door.

"How'd you have time to make the sandwich?" asked Luis, one of Darrell's teammates.

"What?"

"If you were late. How'd you have time to make the sandwich?"

"Just forget it," Harold snapped.

Luis shook his head and wolfed down another fork of spaghetti.

"So how's your grandma feeling?" Darrell asked.

Harold shrugged and bit into his sandwich.

"Got any plans after school today? We got our final match of the season against Zamora High. You should come."

"Nah. I gotta go home," Harold replied. He was anxious to check on Grandma. Besides, he hated Darrell's wrestling matches. He never had anyone to sit with. And watching the athletes with their friends and families cheering them on always left Harold feeling lonely and a little bit jealous.

"C'mon man," Darrell persisted. "Maybe it'll take your mind off things. I bet Cindy'll be there."

"So?" Harold replied.

"I saw you starin' at her during English class today," Darrell said with a grin. "Don't try actin' like you weren't."

"Did you see how she didn't look back?" Harold answered. He knew he was being grumpy, but he didn't care.

"I don't know. She seemed real worried about you last week. The girl was nearly *crying* about your grandma."

Harold grunted and took another bite of his sandwich. *Cindy's worried about Grandma, not me*, he figured. Even if she was concerned last week, that was before he'd made a fool of himself in front of her at SuperFoods and in class. Now she wouldn't even look at him.

"Whatever. I got more important things to worry about," he said.

Darrell looked puzzled, but he let the topic drop. The boys ate in silence then, Darrell with his plate of meatballs and pasta, and Harold with the rest of his crushed sandwich. Soon the table was talking about the upcoming wrestling match.

"So you ready, Mercer?" asked Kevin, a light-skinned junior with a shaved head and the hint of a mustache. He was the best wrestler on Bluford's team.

Darrell grinned. "You know it! I gotta keep my streak goin'."

"That's what I'm talkin' about!" Kevin hollered as he brought down his fist on the table, making the trays jump and clatter. "Coach says if you keep it up, maybe *you'll* be captain by junior year." Kevin sat back in his chair and patted his stomach. "But then again, you'll never be as good as me."

The guys laughed and a few elbowed Darrell playfully, knocking Harold's plastic sandwich bag on the floor. Harold rolled his eyes.

Once Darrell was as shy and awkward as him, hiding each day from Tyray Hobbs, the biggest bully in their class. But a couple of months ago, Darrell used a wrestling move and broke Tyray's wrist in a fight in the middle of the crowded cafeteria. Since then, Tyray left Darrell alone, and Darrell had grown popular.

And I just grew fatter, Harold thought bitterly. *Why am I even sitting here?*

"Seriously, man. You should come," Darrell continued once the laughter had died down. "My family's coming. You could sit with them if you want."

Anger flared deep in Harold's chest. He knew Darrell felt sorry for him, and he hated it. *I don't need you or your family*, he thought. The words boiled inside him.

"Guys, tell Harold he should come," Darrell said.

The table suddenly grew silent. Agonizing seconds passed in silence. Harold wanted to kill Darrell for putting him on the spot like this. Couldn't he see how embarrassing it was?

Finally, Kevin spoke up. "Yeah. Absolutely. You should come, bro."

Harold's face burned with shame. He grabbed his backpack and stood up.

"Thanks, but I got stuff to do."

"C'mon, Harold, don't be like that," Darrell protested. "I was just trying to help."

Harold kicked his chair in and stormed off.

* * *

After school, Harold lumbered back toward his apartment. He was still fuming at what happened in the cafeteria.

I don't need Cindy or Darrell, he thought bitterly as he neared Super-Foods. *I don't need anybody.*

As he passed, he spotted his reflection in the store window. He noticed his full, round face and the creases where the straps of his backpack dug into the soft flesh of his shoulder. Sweat was beginning to stain his dark blue T-shirt under his arms and across his round stomach. It's what always happened when he walked.

"What up, fat boy?" Rodney's words mocked him.

Who am I kidding? I do need help. Harold thought bitterly. The events of the past few days flashed like lightning in his mind. Grandma's wounds, the stacks of unpaid bills, the mysterious envelope with his name on it. Harold's stomach churned as the familiar questions haunted him again.

What if Grandma doesn't get better?

What if we can't pay the bills?

What's gonna happen to us?

"A man's got to think about the future." Londell's advice suddenly made sense. Harold pictured him with his wad of money and confident swagger.

That's what I gotta do, he thought with sudden determination. Next to his reflection was a sign he'd seen in the SuperFoods window before: *Help Wanted.*

Harold remembered how Grandma told him not to get a job. But now it seemed like the only thing he could do. If Grandma couldn't pay the bills, they would have nowhere to live. And if he had money, he could afford all the medical supplies she needed. No more cheap bandages. No more borrowing money from drug dealers.

Minutes later, Harold stood in the personnel office of SuperFoods talking to George Marshall. He was the store manager, a stocky man about forty years old, with a face that reminded Harold of a bulldog.

"Ever had a job before?" he asked.

43

"No sir," Harold answered nervously.

Mr. Marshall talked very fast, as if he was needed urgently somewhere else.

"Live nearby?"

"Yes sir. Just up the street and around the corner."

Mr. Marshall took off his glasses and looked Harold over.

"You go to school?"

"Yes. I'm a freshman at Bluford, sir."

"Live with your parents?"

"No, sir. With my grandmother."

Mr. Marshall frowned. "I'll need a note from her. Is that a problem?"

Harold shook his head. "No."

Mr. Marshall sighed. "You're too young to be a cashier. Stock boy. Minimum wage. That's all I got."

"I'll take it!" Harold exclaimed. "I mean, thank you, sir." Harold could not hide his excitement. Finally he'd be able to help Grandma pay for everything.

"I'll need you three days a week," Mr. Marshall barked, ignoring Harold's enthusiasm. "Monday, Wednesday, Friday from three to six. I expect you to be on time and ready to work. You can start Wednesday," he said, leading Harold out of the office. "And wear a clean shirt," he snapped.

Harold ran out the front door of SuperFoods. He couldn't wait to tell Grandma about his new job. She'd object at first, but he was sure he could convince her that this was a good idea. He would help with the bills and still be home in time to make dinner and finish his homework. Then Grandma could concentrate on getting better.

Harold was about to turn up his block when he heard a familiar voice holler, "There's my boy!"

It was Londell James. He was parked at the curb in a gold Nissan sedan with deep tinted windows and sparkling rims that looked brand new. He seemed to be waiting for someone.

"How's your grandma doin'?"

Harold shrugged.

"Not so good, huh?" Londell said between drags of his cigarette. "No groceries today?"

"Nah," said Harold, embarrassed at the memory of the checkout line. "I got a job, you know, so I can take care of things from now on." For some reason, he wanted Londell to be impressed.

"For real? Where you workin'?"

"Here. At SuperFoods."

Londell smirked. "Let me guess. For

minimum wage, right?"

"Yeah, *so?*" said Harold defensively.

Londell shook his head as if he'd just heard bad news. "Man, you're better than that."

"What do you mean?" Harold asked, surprised that Londell seemed to praise him.

Londell flicked his cigarette and checked his rearview mirror. "I don't want to see you get taken advantage of. Smart kid like you could be somethin'. Be successful. Make enough money to take care of himself. You can't do that workin' in a grocery store."

Harold hadn't thought about it like that.

"I just want to make sure you get what you deserve," Londell continued, his sharp, dark eyes shifting from the rearview mirror to Harold, then back to the mirror.

Harold's head was spinning. Moments ago he'd felt happy and relieved. Now he wondered if he'd made a mistake by taking the job at SuperFoods.

Londell sat up in his seat and put the car into drive. "It's your life, though," he said, preparing to pull away.

"But what else could I do?"

"You could work for me," Londell suggested. "I'll pay you three times what you'll make at this broke-down store. And," he added, leaning toward Harold for emphasis, "you'd have a *future*."

Harold was stunned. No matter what Grandma said, he respected Londell. No one laughed at him, and he didn't seem scared of anything. But Harold knew there was no way he could work for a drug dealer. All his life, Grandma told him about how drugs destroyed the families in their neighborhood, including Londell's. He even knew kids at Bluford, like Bobby Wallace, who'd gotten hooked. He didn't want any part of that.

"No thanks," Harold stammered. "I-I mean . . . I'm not like that."

"Like what?" Londell asked defensively, with a slight flash of anger. "Like me? Like my brother? You think you're better than us?"

Harold looked nervously at the ground. "No! I didn't mean nothin' like that. It's just, I can't, you know, I couldn't—"

"You'd be surprised at what you can do if you need to," Londell interrupted, his eyes intense and dark. "Maybe we're more alike than you think."

47

Harold felt a chill run down his spine. Something about the way Londell was talking frightened him. But he also felt a rush of excitement, as if he was about to learn a secret.

"None of us got parents, Harold," Londell said in a deep, rumbling voice. His words seemed to creep into Harold's skin and down his spine. "All those boys you saw the other day—Jupiter, Bug, Keenan, all my boys—we on our own. Might as well be orphans. Just like you."

Harold remembered the boy he saw outside SuperFoods with Jupiter. The thought of such a young boy without someone to protect him filled Harold with an awful, sickening sadness. And yet, if not for Grandma, he'd be in the same position.

"We ain't like those kids you see at Bluford, worryin' about class, parents all savin' up for college," Londell said with a bitter laugh. "No one's lookin' out for us. *I* take care o' my boys. *I* give 'em a family. *I* give 'em money. And a *future*. You think on *that*."

Suddenly, Harold felt a powerful shove from behind that sent his backpack flying to the sidewalk.

"Out my way, sausage," growled

Jupiter. "Yo Londell, why *he* here?"

Jupiter got into the car next to his brother and slammed the door, tossing a brown paper bag on the seat. He was wearing a crisp white basketball jersey and dark blue jeans. A small diamond earring sparkled below his perfect, tightly braided hair.

Londell glared angrily at Jupiter. "Under the seat!" he growled. "How many times I gotta tell you?"

Jupiter shoved the bag underneath the front seat of the car.

"Gotta go, Harold," Londell continued. "Think about what I said. I won't be around here for a while, so . . . the playground on 25th Street. You can find me there."

Londell glanced at the front door of SuperFoods and shook his head at Harold.

"Good luck with your new job," he said. Then he hit the gas, squealing the tires as he took off down the street.

Harold stood, frozen in place, caught between Londell's fading taillights and Mr. Marshall's angry stare, which beamed at him through the tall glass doors of SuperFoods.

Chapter 4

Crunch!

The ten-pound bag of cat litter slammed to the floor and tore open, sending a dusty cascade of sand across aisle seven of SuperFoods.

"C'mon, Davis!" Mr. Marshall barked as he stormed up the aisle with a clipboard in his hand. "What's *wrong* with you?"

"Sorry, Mr. Marshall," Harold answered, trying to keep the rest of the bags from falling off the overloaded cart he was pushing down the narrow aisle. It was the second time today that Harold knocked something over.

At least it's not jars of salsa, he thought wearily. *I won't have to mop anything this time.*

Harold was exhausted. He'd been working at SuperFoods for a full week, unloading crates and stocking shelves for three hours at a time. It was hard work, made worse by Mr. Marshall's constant frustration at how slow and clumsy Harold was.

"You keep this up, and I'm gonna have to charge you, son," Mr. Marshall said, shaking his head with irritation. "Go on, clean it up!"

"Yes, sir," Harold answered, grabbing the broom and dustpan he'd needed almost every day. He was proud he was working, but he was exhausted from his new schedule. On workdays, he'd stop home right after school to check on Grandma. Then he'd rush to Super-Foods, spend several hours lifting crates of canned food and cat litter, and head home to make dinner.

At first Grandma refused to sign the papers Mr. Marshall needed to hire him. It was only when he told her he wanted to be more independent that she reluctantly let him take the job.

"You're growin' up right before my eyes, child," she said with a mixture of pride and sadness. *"I suppose I shouldn't stand in the way of that."* He felt guilty for lying, but he'd seen her hospital bills and knew he had to help out.

"Almost forgot, it's payday," said Mr. Marshall, as Harold swept up the last of the cat litter. "You can pick up your check in my office. Want me to cash it for you?"

"Yeah," Harold replied with an eager smile. He was excited to get his first paycheck.

"Didn't think you'd last two days," said Mr. Marshall. "Thought you'd be trouble, like that other guy I saw you with."

Harold knew he was talking about Londell.

"You're clumsy, but you work hard," Mr. Marshall added thoughtfully. "I've had bad luck with stock boys in the past. Glad to see you're trying your best."

"Thanks, Mr. Marshall," Harold replied with pride. "I won't let you down."

At 6:10, Harold dashed out the front door of SuperFoods. He was running late and still had to make dinner, finish his homework, and change Grandma's bandage.

At least I got paid, he thought with excitement as he tore open the envelope Mr. Marshall had given him. He fished out the bills and counted.

This can't be right! he thought, counting again. He had forty-eight dollars and some change. *Where's the rest?*

Harold grabbed the pay stub that was in the envelope. At the top, it said he'd earned $65.25. But then there was a list of "deductions" like taxes and other things Harold didn't understand. In the end, he'd take home only $48.20.

Harold crumpled the pay stub in frustration. He had barely any money, and already it was being taken away. Even if he worked all year, he realized, he still wouldn't be able to pay the bills he'd seen.

What about groceries? he wondered, suddenly feeling hopeless. Then there were the tests, medications, and procedures he knew Grandma would need. And he'd need money for his own things too, clothes and shoes and lunch. How could he pay for everything?

"You can't do that workin' in a grocery store." Londell's words haunted him as he crossed the street to his apartment.

* * *

"I'm here, Grandma!" Harold yelled as he unlocked the door. "Sorry I'm late."

He was surprised to find Mr. Harris chopping vegetables in the kitchen. A large pot of water boiled on the stove, and the room was filled with a rich buttery scent that made Harold's mouth water.

"I was startin' to worry about you, child!" Grandma yelled from the living room.

"Did you test your blood, Grandma?" Harold asked as he looked for Grandma's Glucometer.

She was sitting on the couch watching television. Her eyelids sagged sleepily. A fresh white bandage covered her wound. "Mr. Harris is cookin' dinner for us tonight. Ain't that nice of him?" she said.

"I had tonight off and figured I'd stop by," said Mr. Harris as he sliced an orange-colored squash into small cubes. "She tested her blood, and we changed that bandage. Thought maybe you could use a hand."

"You have no idea," Harold replied, grateful he didn't have to spend another evening trying to cook dinner with Grandma yelling instructions at him from the other room.

Mr. Harris smiled and tossed a handful of brightly colored vegetables into a shallow dish.

Harold hadn't seen him since Grandma came back from the hospital. Already the two days he'd stayed in Mr.

Harris's apartment seemed like a foggy memory. Harold had left each morning for the hospital and returned at night to find a plate of food waiting on the kitchen counter. Mr. Harris would be sitting on the couch, quietly reading or writing in his notebook. Harold had been too upset to talk much.

"I've been meaning to thank you. For all you did," Harold said. "We didn't mean to bother you with our problems."

"Glad to help," he replied. "You hungry?"

"Starving," Harold admitted, looking at the bowl of strange vegetables. "What's for dinner?"

"Pasta and roasted veggies. Eggplant. Butternut squash."

"Sounds good," Harold lied, not wanting to admit that he hated vegetables.

"Don't look so excited," Mr. Harris said with a knowing smile.

"Sorry. I never had eggplant before. Or squash," Harold admitted, feeling silly. He watched Mr. Harris chop the vegetables into neat, even cubes. The knife blade moved in a silver blur across the cutting board. It reminded him of a cooking show Grandma used to watch on TV.

"Where'd you learn to cook like that?" Harold asked.

"Overseas," Mr. Harris said vaguely. "Let's set the table."

Harold grabbed the plates and silverware, while Mr. Harris carried in the food. Once the table was ready, Harold brought Grandma her wooden crutches.

"Dinner's ready, Grandma," he said softly. "Let me help you up."

"Oh, baby, I think I'll eat here tonight. I'm just so *tired*," she said, patting his face. "You look tired too. They're not working you too hard at SuperFoods, are they?" she added. "I don't want you running yourself ragged. You got your studies to worry about."

"I'm okay," he insisted. "I'll get you some food."

Harold carefully filled Grandma's plate and took it to her. Then he sat at the table with Mr. Harris and devoured his dinner hungrily. He was surprised at how much he liked the sweet orange squash and meaty chunks of eggplant.

"That was good," he said, wiping his mouth with a napkin. "Really."

"It's a good meal for your grandma. Healthy," Mr. Harris said.

"The doctors gave us a list of foods, but I don't know how to cook most of 'em," Harold admitted, looking over at

Grandma, who was scratching her leg.

"Tell you what," Mr. Harris replied, folding his napkin neatly on the table. "I'm going shopping Saturday. Why don't you come with me? Maybe I can help you make sense of that list. It's important that your grandma eats right," he paused, staring directly at Harold. "You, too."

Harold nodded, suddenly embarrassed about his weight. For a moment, he thought maybe Mr. Harris was teasing him. But his face was sincere.

"How's your dinner, Mrs. Rose?" he called into the living room.

"Why it's wonderful, Markus, thank you!" she answered. "Now don't y'all worry about me. You just go 'head and enjoy yourselves. And Harold, don't you forget about your homework. I don't want this job of yours interferin' with school!" she added.

"I *know*, Grandma," he groaned, thinking of his small paycheck and the mountain of homework he'd yet to start.

I know.

* * *

After dinner, Harold washed the dishes and found a cutting board Mr.

Harris left in their apartment. He went down the hall to return it, knocking gently on the door.

"It's me, Mr. Harris," Harold said. "You forgot something."

Mr. Harris opened the door. "Thanks, Harold," he said, taking the cutting board. Behind him, Harold saw the glow of a computer screen surrounded by a stack of books. "C'mon in. I'm just doing some homework and could use a break."

"Homework?"

"That's right. You're not the only one in class right now," Mr. Harris said, returning the cutting board to his kitchen.

Harold was confused but didn't want to seem nosey. *Wasn't he too old to be in school?*

Though Harold spent two days in the apartment, he didn't realize how neat it was until now. A small couch and leather chair were arranged against the wall. Opposite them was a large wooden bookshelf. Next to it was the computer desk. A thick textbook called *Aviation Mechanics* was open face-down in front of the computer. Beside it was a stack of notebooks. The top one was open, its page filled with small angular handwriting.

Harold spotted photographs on the

wall he'd barely noticed the nights Grandma was in the hospital. One showed Mr. Harris standing in front of a large black helicopter, the two massive blades sagging just over his head. He was wearing beige and brown fatigues. Behind him, a dry sandy desert stretched to the horizon. Another photo showed Mr. Harris walking down a narrow street made of rounded gray stones. A street sign over Mr. Harris's head had a strange word Harold couldn't pronounce: *Landstuhl.*

"That's Germany. I was stationed there for a while," said Mr. Harris, straightening up his desk.

Harold studied the picture. He couldn't imagine being in such a faraway place. He'd never been more than an hour from the city.

"What's it like there?" he asked eagerly.

"It's beautiful."

Gotta be better than here, Harold thought as he glanced at a photo of a group of men posed in front of a helicopter. Some were holding large guns.

"Who are these guys?" Harold asked.

"That's my crew," said Mr. Harris. "And my chopper."

"You *owned* that helicopter?" Harold asked.

Mr. Harris chuckled. "No. I mean, I took care of that helicopter. I was the crew chief. I repaired it. I made sure the men inside were flying a safe aircraft."

"Did you get into actual fights?" Harold asked. "I mean, were you in battles and stuff?" He imagined Mr. Harris in fatigues, ducking gunfire and racing to reach his downed chopper and injured men.

"It's not like what you see in the movies," Mr. Harris replied gravely.

"Yeah, but still," Harold persisted, his mind drifting to a place without Londell or Mr. Marshall, without endless stacks of bills, without the social worker's questions. "Don't you miss it sometimes?"

"No, I don't," he replied flatly. "I'm glad to be home. I'm in college now."

"*College*?" Harold asked. "That's why you doin' homework?"

"That's right," Mr. Harris smiled proudly. "Thirty-six years old, and I'm finally getting my degree."

"Cool," Harold said, glancing back at the photo of the men and their guns. "Maybe I should join the Marines."

Mr. Harris shut his textbook and

glared at Harold. "Maybe you should just go straight to college."

* * *

That night, Harold couldn't relax. Alone in his bedroom, he counted and recounted his pay, scribbling numbers on a notepad, searching for a way to make them add up.

It's hopeless, Harold thought miserably. Even if he worked an extra day per week, he couldn't afford groceries. *And what about the other bills Grandma was hiding?*

At 3:17, Harold gave up on sleep and got out of bed. He could hear Grandma snoring gently from her room as he went into the kitchen to get some water. In the shadowy living room, he noticed Grandma's stack of papers near the couch.

"I don't want you snooping around. That's my business," Grandma's words bounced through his head. He remembered the envelope he'd seen with his name on it. Was it in the pile? The stack of papers seemed to call him.

It's my business too, Grandma! He wanted to say. *How can I help if I don't know what's happening?*

Moving quietly, Harold crept over to the sofa. His heart was racing. He was about to reach for the stack when a siren screamed outside. Harold sat motionless as it passed, listening for several minutes to make sure Grandma was still asleep. He'd never disobeyed her on something so serious.

But that envelope has my name on it! I deserve to know what it says.

His hands started moving then. In the darkened living room, Harold rifled through Grandma's papers.

There were more bills, even more than before. They were nearly $10,000 in debt. There was even a threatening note from a collection agency. And buried in the middle of the stack was the envelope. Harold held his breath and opened it:

Dear Mrs. Davis,

The state must be advised as to custody or guardianship of your grandson, Harold Davis, 15, in the event of your disability, death, or if you are otherwise unable to provide for him.

Please complete the attached form and return it to our offices promptly. **Should no guardian be available, the state will take custody of Harold Davis until permanent placement can be found.**

"*No!*" Harold gasped. He flipped to the next page. Grandma had filled out the top portion, but under "Appointed Guardian," the form was blank.

"*Do you have any other family, Harold? Is there someone you can stay with?*" The social worker's questions taunted him.

Harold reread the letter, staring again at the bold words: "*the state will take custody of Harold Davis.*"

Harold trembled as the truth crushed down on him. With their bills, Grandma couldn't afford to live in the apartment. There was no way she could provide for him. The collection agency would come and take everything. There was no way out.

Harold gripped the carpet and let out a soft cry as Londell's words crashed through his mind like thunder.

"*We're all on our own. Might as well be orphans.*"

Harold buried his face in Grandma's

blanket and sobbed, the scent of her perfume filling him with a deep, aching loneliness. He wished he could crawl into her lap and hear her say that everything would be okay, like she had so many times. He wanted to be eight years old again, home from school with a scraped knee and Grandma as strong as ever. But those days were long gone.

I'm not a kid anymore, Harold thought desperately. He felt like something had ripped deep inside his body, leaving him bleeding and defenseless, though no one else could tell.

Harold staggered back to his room, his shoulders heaving with waves of grief. He grabbed the candy bar Londell had given him and tore into the wrapper. Harold knew he shouldn't eat candy, but he let the sweet, dark chocolate fill his mouth as he collapsed on his bed.

I got no other choice, he thought, rocking back and forth.

It doesn't matter what I want. I got no other choice.

The following day after school, Harold walked to SuperFoods and straight into Mr. Marshall's office.

"I quit," he said plainly, and walked out.

Chapter 5

Harold's hands were wet with sweat as he climbed aboard the bus to 25th Street. He'd taken the bus many times, but never to where Londell told him to go, a neighborhood Grandma often warned him about.

Twenty minutes later, the bus hissed to a stop, and Harold climbed down onto the dirty sidewalk. The streets were eerily quiet. There were no kids running home from school, no mothers carrying groceries, no delivery trucks or people walking dogs. All Harold could see were blocks of small dingy houses huddled close together. On the corner was the burnt-out skeleton of a bar.

Harold headed up the block, looking for the playground Londell mentioned. He was amazed at how desolate 25th Street was. Many windows were boarded up, as if the houses were hiding their eyes. Rooftops sagged at dangerous angles. Crumbling porches gave way to tiny yards of dirt and garbage.

Harold passed a rusty car whose tires had long been removed. Up ahead, a skinny cat scurried across the street toward a spilled garbage can. Harold walked faster, nearly tripping over an empty beer bottle, which rolled noisily into the gutter.

It's dead here, he thought as he hurried toward the playground where three figures stood on the corner, watching him.

Harold swallowed hard. He felt as if he was about to cross into a place of no return. His knees trembled. *This is it,* he thought, forcing himself forward.

"What'chu want, sausage?" Jupiter snapped as he stepped forward from the group.

"Yeah," added the tall thin boy standing behind him. His top lip was swollen. The youngest boy, whom Harold remembered from SuperFoods, swung his arms absentmindedly.

"I'm lookin' for Londell," said Harold, trying to sound confident. "He said I could find him here."

Jupiter charged up to Harold, his

face just inches away. "Well, he *ain't* here," he growled, jabbing a sharp finger into Harold's chest, "so go back to Grandma's." Harold could feel his hot breath on his face.

"I gotta see Londell," Harold insisted, holding Jupiter's gaze. "It's important."

"Yo Keenan, this boy think Londell his friend or somethin'," Jupiter said with a smirk to the tall, thin boy. "Maybe he got a crush on him."

This was a mistake, Harold thought. *They're gonna jump me and leave me for dead.*

"Nah, man. I just gotta talk to him," Harold said quickly. "Londell said—"

"I don't care *what* he said!" Jupiter snarled, jabbing Harold's chest again. "He ain't here, and when *he* ain't here, *I'm* in charge. This *my* corner. So get off."

"Yeah," said Keenan. "This is Joop's corner."

"I'm not leaving till I see Londell," Harold insisted, bracing himself for another shove.

Jupiter's eyes blazed with anger. "How 'bout I *make* you leave, boy?"

"Joop, I'm hungry!" the young boy suddenly blurted, distracting Jupiter long enough for Harold to back away.

67

"When we gonna eat?"

"Quit botherin' me, Bug." Jupiter snapped, shaking his head in frustration. "Now you see why we call him that, Kee? He never stop buggin'. You'll eat when Londell get here," Jupiter added, turning back to the boy.

"But I'm hungry *now*," Bug persisted, squirming and holding his stomach. Up close, Bug looked even younger to Harold, maybe just eight years old. He had a small round face and wide puppy-like eyes. His short, stocky body reminded Harold of a baby bulldog.

"What'chu want me to do? Make you dinner or something?" Jupiter said with an annoyed glare. "You'll eat when Londell git here."

"But I'm *starvin'*, Joop," he complained. "And we ain't even start work yet."

Jupiter rolled his eyes. "Boy, this ain't no foster home. Getcha own food if you that hungry."

Harold cringed. He remembered what Londell said about each of them. *No family.* The words took on new meaning as he looked at the hungry kid next to him.

"I got a sandwich," Harold said quietly, reaching into his backpack.

"Shut up!" Jupiter snapped.

"For real?" said Bug, his eyes widening.

Harold smiled. "You like peanut butter and jelly?"

"Yeah!" he answered, bouncing over to Harold's side.

"Yo, this boy just pulled out a sandwich!" exclaimed Jupiter between fits of laughter. "Bet he got a whole damn dinner in there, too!"

Keenan laughed and slapped Jupiter's hand in agreement. "Yeah. He look like he hidin' a whole chicken in there. Maybe a turkey."

"What's for dessert, yo!" Jupiter screamed, cackling loudly. He and Keenan were laughing so hard they could barely stand.

Jupiter was nothing like the kid Harold remembered from middle school. Back then, he was almost as quiet as Harold. Everything changed the afternoon in seventh grade when his father was murdered. The principal had barged into class and asked Jupiter to come to the office. Seconds later, Harold heard Jupiter's scream in the hallway. The sound made Mrs. Kirby, their teacher, drop the chalk in her hand. They were twelve years old.

Harold had tried to become Jupiter's

friend after that; he knew how hard it was to grow up without a dad. But Jupiter returned to school ten days later with a wild look in his eyes that hadn't been there before. It was impossible to talk to Jupiter after that. He started acting out in school, fighting with classmates and even cursing at teachers if they called on him in class. Once, in a fit of rage, he punched a gymnasium window, shattering the glass and cutting his hand badly. Harold stayed away from him after that.

Now, standing at the edge of the abandoned playground, Harold saw that same wild look still lurking in Jupiter's eyes.

"Ain't nobody want you here," Jupiter continued.

"Yo, Joop, they comin' out already!" Keenan interrupted, pointing down the street. In the distance, someone was walking toward them.

"Who's that?" Harold asked nervously.

"Junkies," said Bug between bites of his sandwich. There was a smear of jelly on his chin.

The sun was beginning to set and Harold squinted toward the orange glare. The figure was getting closer. It was a small, thin man. His dirty clothes hung limply from his body.

This is crazy! Harold thought. *I shouldn't be here.*

"I gotta go," he whispered out loud. He looked at Bug, who wandered toward an old house with boarded-up windows.

Suddenly, Harold heard the low rumble of a car approaching.

"Londell comin'!" Bug exclaimed as the gold Nissan pulled up to the curb. Londell rolled down his window and smiled at Harold.

"Well, look who it is," he said with an approving nod.

"Hey," Harold said, feeling a bit safer with Londell nearby.

"Yo Londell, why you tell *him* to come here?" said Jupiter, nudging Harold as he jumped into the front seat of the car.

Londell kept his eyes on Harold. "Get out, Joop," he said. "C'mere, Harold."

"Why you gotta be like that?" Jupiter protested.

Londell tossed him a brown paper bag. "Get to work. We got a line already."

Jupiter climbed out and shot Harold an angry glare, shoving the paper bag down the front of his pants.

Harold tried to stay calm as he sat next to Londell, but he felt like hiding under the seat and covering his eyes.

"Yo, Londell," said Bug, circling over to the passenger window with a big grin. "Whatchu bring for dinner?"

"Hey Bug," Londell answered. "How 'bout a cheeseburger?"

Londell reached into the back seat and handed Bug a bag of fast food.

"Thanks!" Bug said, taking the bag and running back to the playground.

"How's that lip, Kee?" Londell shouted with an amused expression.

Keenan frowned. "All right," he answered meekly.

Londell checked his rearview mirror. Harold thought he looked slightly nervous. "I'll be back in a couple hours, Joop," he hollered. "Make sure Bug takes care of those lights."

Harold was relieved when Londell pulled away from the curb. He could see a few more people making their way down the street toward the corner. In the glare of the setting sun, he couldn't see their faces, only the way they were walking. Some moved quickly, urgently, while others dragged themselves wearily. Harold shivered and locked the door.

"So, what's up? You need something?" Londell asked, checking the mirror again.

Harold hesitated. *I don't think I can do*

this, he thought to himself, wiping the sweat from his forehead. He felt nauseous, and his head was starting to throb.

Londell put his hand on Harold's shoulder. "Relax. *You* ain't got nothin' to worry about."

Harold knew what he was about to do was wrong, that it would break Grandma's heart, that it went against everything she taught. But there was no escaping the bills and that letter. He had to do something before it was too late and the social worker came to take him away.

"I need a job, but—"

"Thought you had a job," Londell said, glancing at the cell phone in his lap.

"I do. I mean, I did," Harold swallowed hard. "I quit."

"What happened?" said Londell, pulling out a cigarette from his leather jacket.

"I guess I did some thinkin'. I realized you were right. I gotta take care of myself. And my grandma. I can't do that at SuperFoods."

Londell nodded thoughtfully. "I knew you was smart," he said with an approving smile.

"I don't think I can stand on that corner," Harold blurted.

73

Londell laughed. "Don't worry. I ain't gonna put you on the corner. You're gonna be my delivery boy."

"What's that?" Harold asked cautiously.

"I got certain . . ." Londell paused as if he was searching for the right word, "*customers* I deliver to personally. Regulars who spend a lot of money. It's easy. I give you the packages. Then you deliver 'em to the addresses. The customers give you the money, and you bring the cash back to me. Think you can handle that?"

"Maybe," said Harold. He still wasn't sure, but at least it sounded better than the corner.

Harold stared out the window, watching block after block of lifeless houses pass by. Then they crossed into a different neighborhood. A few trees appeared, then grassy front yards. The houses began to look alive again, with chairs set out on the porches and even a few flower pots here and there. Two kids riding bicycles crossed in front of Londell's car.

"Look, Harold. As long as you're not stupid, you'll be fine. Just keep your head down and your eyes open. I'll pay you fifty bucks a day. Shouldn't take you more than a couple of hours from start to finish."

Fifty bucks a day! Harold thought with excitement. With that money, he realized, he could pay for Grandma's emergency room bill by himself in just a few weeks.

"And to start you off, here's a little something." Londell handed Harold a crisp fifty-dollar bill. "For being such a smart kid, and for trusting me."

Londell pulled up in front of a small white house with green shutters.

"Where are we?" Harold asked.

"At your first delivery."

"*Here?*" he asked. Harold was surprised. The house was nothing like the boarded-up buildings near the playground. It looked like a nice home. Maybe a family lived inside.

"That's right. Business is everywhere," Londell said, reaching underneath his seat and pulling out a brown paper bag. He opened it, checking the contents, and handed it to Harold.

"Bring this up to the front door and ask for Shawn. He'll give you $100; you give him the bag. Then bring the money back to me."

Harold's stomach trembled, and his heart thumped heavily beneath his sweaty T-shirt.

"How's he gonna know what I'm here for?" he asked nervously. He didn't ask what was in the brown paper bags. *I don't wanna know*, he thought. *I don't ever want to know.*

"Oh, he'll know," Londell said, glancing at his cell phone again. "He's been waiting for me all day."

Londell's face turned serious. "One more thing: never give a customer his package till you have the cash in your hand. You make sure it's all there, *then* you hand it to him. Not before. Understand?"

"Yeah," said Harold.

Londell's voice lowered. "The money's on you, Harold. And the guy I work for, he don't like excuses. Don't you *ever* come back to me short on what you owe. Y'hear?"

Harold nodded somberly. For a moment, Londell's eyes flashed with the same wildness Jupiter's had. But then it was gone.

"Go on. Whatcha waitin' for?"

Harold climbed out of the car and walked up to the front door, glancing back nervously at Londell. From the doorstep, he could hear the muffled sound of a TV.

76

A small sports car sat in the driveway.

Harold knocked on the door. After a few seconds, a clean-shaven man appeared.

"You Shawn?" Harold asked.

The man nodded. He was wearing a blue button-down shirt and beige pants. His eyes were slightly red, but otherwise he didn't look at all like what Harold had expected. Shawn glanced at Harold, then at Londell before handing Harold one hundred dollars.

Harold counted the money, handed him the bag and quickly returned to Londell's car.

"That's it?" Harold asked with a wave of relief.

"That's it. Not so bad, right?"

Harold smiled. *Not bad at all*, he thought.

"I take care of my boys, Harold. Long as you do your job and keep your mouth shut, I'll make sure you get the money you need. Understand?"

Harold nodded, and Londell shifted the car into drive.

"So, you in?" he asked, his eyes locked on Harold's.

"Yeah," said Harold, clutching the fifty-dollar bill near his heart. "I'm in."

Chapter 6

Londell dropped Harold off at the corner of his block.

"Thanks for the ride," Harold said. "And the money."

"No problem. I'll see you tomorrow after school."

Harold bounded up the street, smiling to himself. For the first time in weeks, he felt like he was in control. Working for Londell didn't seem that dangerous: the man he delivered to seemed pretty normal. Besides, it wasn't like he was selling drugs to kids. And once he made enough money, he could quit and go back to a normal job.

Suddenly, Harold heard a familiar voice.

"*Harold?*"

He turned to see Cindy walking just a half block behind him. She was wearing sweatpants and a loose-fitting T-shirt. A SuperFoods shopping bag hung from her fingers, and Her forehead was creased with worry.

"Where were you? Grandma Rose said you were working at SuperFoods, but I went there, and they told me you didn't work there anymore."

Harold cringed. She had avoided him since he'd spoken to Londell. There was no way he could tell her where he'd been.

"I quit that job. Me and Mr. Marshall didn't get along," he lied.

Cindy caught up with him then. Her amber eyes focused on him like twin spotlights.

"Why are you doing that?" she asked, shaking her head sadly.

"What?"

"*Lying*," she said, wiping her eyes as she spoke. "I saw you get outta Londell's car. We both know what he does, Harold. Don't treat me like I'm stupid."

There was a sorrow in her voice that made him ache inside.

"It's not what you think," Harold pleaded. "He's not that bad."

Cindy rolled her eyes. "He's a drug dealer, Harold! That's all I need to know."

"You don't understand, Cindy," Harold

said defensively.

"No, *you* don't understand!" Cindy yelled. "My mom used to date a drug dealer, remember? I saw what drugs do to people. I watched Bobby Wallace almost die in front of me from an overdose. Don't tell me I don't understand."

Harold knew what Cindy was talking about, but Londell was different. He looked out for his boys. Harold pictured Bug munching happily on his cheeseburger.

"Londell's not like that, Cindy. He takes care of us—"

"*Us?*" Cindy's eyes widened with disbelief. "You mean you're *workin'* for him?"

"Look, he's helping me, okay?" Harold admitted, thinking of the money in his pocket and the piles of bills he'd seen last night. "I need his help right now. I can't explain it all. Just trust me."

Cindy nodded and stepped away from him, as if she had just given up. Her eyes glistened with tears.

"Well, I guess you don't need *my* help anymore," she sighed, handing him the bag from SuperFoods and walking away.

Harold looked inside and saw two packages of the expensive bandages Grandma needed for her leg. He knew she'd bought them for him.

"Cindy, don't be like that," Harold called to her, but she rushed up the street and dashed into their building. "*Cindy!*"

The door slammed, and Harold was alone on the street.

* * *

"I'm home, Grandma!" Harold yelled as he walked into the apartment.

"Where you *been*, child?!" Grandma shouted angrily from the couch. "You're late. I was startin' to get worried!"

Harold had been so busy with Londell and Cindy, he'd forgotten to look at the clock. It was a half hour later than when he usually got back from Super-Foods. His mind raced for an excuse.

"We got a big shipment," he said, dumping his backpack on the floor. "Mr. Marshall asked if I could stay a little later to help out. He likes my work and wants to increase my schedule to five days a week, too." Harold hated lying, but he was doing it for the both of them. It was the only way.

Grandma grunted at the news. He knew she wasn't happy.

"Harold, you shoulda called to let me know you were gonna be late," she said, rubbing her leg. "I don't like the idea of you working every day either. Three days a week is plenty for a boy your age."

"But Grandma!" he protested, rushing over to the couch. "He gave me a raise! He said I was a good worker. I swear I'll keep up with my homework. And I'll be home in time to help with dinner."

Grandma arched her eyebrows skeptically. "I don't know, Harold. It seems like an awful lot."

"Please, Grandma!" he persisted, sitting down beside her. "It's important to me. If my grades start slipping, I'll cut back my hours. I promise."

"My goodness," she replied, patting his hand. "I've never heard you so excited. Usually I can't get you out from in front of that TV."

"Guess I'm growing up," he said, forcing himself to smile despite the guilt that clawed invisibly at his chest.

"Well, I suppose it's not the worst thing in the world, having something of your own. Lord knows it can't be good for you, taking care of me all the time." Grandma sighed thoughtfully.

"It's not so bad, Grandma," he replied. He noticed the bruise on her face was fading, and though she still looked tired, her eyes seemed a bit brighter.

As long as you get better, Grandma, he thought to himself. *That's all that matters.*

"Okay, baby," she said reluctantly. "You can tell Mr. Marshall we'll give this new schedule a try. But I'll be checking your homework," she added, pointing her finger sternly. "I know I haven't kept up on that like I should, but school comes first, understand?"

Harold nodded. "I know, Grandma. I know."

* * *

That night, Harold waited for Grandma to fall asleep. He crept into the kitchen and sifted through the neat pile of bills she'd left for him to mail. Harold guessed which ones would be cheapest and carefully sliced them open with a knife. The electric bill was $38.15. Harold removed Grandma's check, replacing it with $40 he made at SuperFoods. He did the same with the phone bill, which was $47.38, sliding in Londell's $50 bill and then carefully resealing the envelopes with tape.

"It's gonna be all right, Grandma," he

whispered out loud, slipping the mail into his backpack. "I'm gonna take care of everything."

* * *

The next morning, Harold woke up early, his heart pounding with nervous energy. He showered and quickly made three ham and cheese sandwiches: one he left in the fridge for Grandma's lunch, the others he stuffed in his backpack. Harold wolfed down two pieces of toast while he finished his English homework. Then he headed out the door, dropping the bills in the mailbox, and walked to school.

All day he watched the clock. As soon as the last bell rang, Harold raced to his locker to unload the books he wouldn't need that night. From the corner of his eye, he spotted Darrell Mercer walking toward him.

Not now, he thought to himself. *I don't have time for this.*

"Yo Harold, what's up with you?" Darrell said quietly, leaning against the wall of lockers.

Harold shrugged. "Nothing. Just busy, that's all."

Darrell looked at him thoughtfully. "Busy? You barely said a word to me all week. If it's what happened in the cafeteria the other day, I'm sorry. You and me, we're boys. You know that."

Harold slammed his locker closed and rolled his eyes. "I gotta go," he said.

"C'mon," Darrell persisted. "What's going on? Why you actin' this way?"

Harold zipped up his backpack and shook his head impatiently. "I told you. I gotta go," he repeated. "I'm late already."

Darrell threw up his hands in frustration. "What do you want me to say? Just tell me and I'll do it."

"Nothing," Harold replied as he turned to leave. "Just stay away from me, Darrell. You're better off."

Harold rushed out the front doors of Bluford High and took the bus to 25th Street. He had to be home by 6:30 or else Grandma would ask questions. The earlier he got to the playground, the faster he could finish up and get home.

Harold quickly made his way down the street past the rows of silent houses. It was warmer than yesterday. Overhead, the mid-March sun heated the neighborhood, filling the air with the thick scent of garbage and burned wood.

Suddenly, Harold heard the sound of shattering glass. Up ahead, he could see someone covering his head and running. Harold gasped and ducked behind a car.

Who is that? he thought fearfully, looking around for something he could use as a weapon.

The crash of shattering glass boomed in the air again, closer this time. Harold peeked around the rusty bumper and saw a familiar young face.

"Bug?" Harold called.

"Hey, Harold!" said Bug with a grin. "What'chu hidin' for?"

Small shards of glass covered Bug's head and the top of his bright yellow backpack. He was holding several rocks in his hand, and a small slingshot made from a rubber band and Y-shaped twig.

"What're you doing?!" Harold cried. "You scared me!"

Bug looked confused. "I'm workin'. Breakin' street lights like Londell said."

"Don't move," said Harold as he brushed glass particles off Bug's clothes. "You gotta be careful. You could cut yourself!" he said sternly.

"Quit it!" Bug said squirming as Harold removed the glass from his hair. "That tickles!"

"Hold still, Bug. I'm serious." Harold turned him around and checked his T-shirt for glass.

"Got any more sandwiches?" Bug asked eagerly.

Harold smiled. "I made one just for you. Ham and cheese," he said.

"For real?" Bug asked excitedly.

"Yeah, for real," said Harold. In the distance, he could see Jupiter and Keenan at the park, sitting on a rusty swing set. "C'mon. Let's go."

"You go to school, Bug?" Harold asked as they continued up the street together.

"Yeah," said Bug with a frown.

"What's wrong? You don't like school?"

Bug shook his head. "I hate it," he said quietly.

"How come?"

Bug shrugged and fiddled with his slingshot.

"I bet you're a smart kid," Harold said.

"My new foster mom say that, too."

"You should listen to her," he replied.

Bug adjusted his backpack. "I guess. But I don't know nobody at school. I'm *always* the new kid. Everybody be teasin' me . . . not like out here."

Harold winced. He'd faced the same

treatment himself in school, but the idea of Bug getting hassled seemed crueler. Bug was just a kid, ready to follow anyone as long as they were friendly. He belonged in a good home and a good school, not on the corner with drug dealers.

"I know it's hard," Harold said, hearing Grandma's advice in his words. "But once the other kids get to know you, you'll be okay. Just don't hit 'em with any of your rocks."

"I won't," Bug said with a chuckle. "Londell say I only gotta go to school for a couple more years anyway, till I'm big like Joop. Then I can work for real."

"What'd he say?" Harold asked, but Bug raced up ahead, stopping directly under a streetlight. Harold watched as Bug squinted, craning his neck backward to examine it.

"Plastic," he mumbled, aiming the slingshot and hurling a small stone at the light.

Thunk. The clear plastic cover cracked but didn't shatter.

"Careful!" Harold yelled protectively, rushing over to him. "Why's Londell got you breakin' lights?"

"So the cops can't see Joop and Kee

when it's dark," Bug explained, as if Harold had asked a silly question. "Can I get my sandwich now? I'm hungry!"

"Sure," said Harold with a sigh, reaching into his backpack. "But you gotta be more careful. Maybe wear a hat or something so that glass doesn't get on you. And no matter what Londell says, you gotta stay in school."

"You gonna be here every day?" Bug asked as he unwrapped his sandwich.

"Maybe," said Harold.

"That's cool," Bug replied between bites of his sandwich. "You nice, Harold."

Moments later, they stepped into the park.

"What's up?" Harold said to Jupiter and Keenan. "Londell around yet?"

"'Sup," Keenan nodded.

"He ain't here," Jupiter said. He had a small bruise on his cheek.

Harold glanced at his watch. It was almost 4:30. "Know what time he'll show up? I gotta get home in a couple hours."

Jupiter shrugged. "He'll be here when he's here. He don't tell me nothin'," he added, his voice slightly bitter.

"Yo Bug, you done wit' those lights yet?" Jupiter shouted. Bug was sitting on a rusty bench, rummaging through his backpack.

"Almost," Bug replied.

"You better finish before it get dark," Jupiter yelled.

"I gotta do my homework," Bug complained with a quick glance at Harold.

"You got work to do, Bug," Jupiter said impatiently. "And if you don't do it, Londell gonna yell at me again. So get movin'."

Bug wandered off, and the park was silent except for the gloomy squeak of the rusty swings. Harold thought about Cindy; how she'd spent what little money she had on his grandmother's bandages. He knew she'd never talk to him again, not after what she'd learned. *Maybe it was best*, he figured, looking at the bleak playground as quiet as a graveyard.

Next to him, Jupiter gazed at a vacant house, tracing the long scar on the back of his hand with his finger. Harold recalled the day back in middle school when Jupiter punched that window, gashing himself and leaving a trail of blood droplets on the basketball court.

"I remember when you did that," Harold said quietly.

"Did what?" Jupiter snapped.

"Cut your hand."

"Oh," he replied, shoving
his pocket. "Yeah." Jupiter
a moment. "They kicked m
after that," he admitted, his voi
ing off.

"You ever gonna go back?" Harold
asked cautiously.

"Nah. I'm supposed to be in Bluford
now, but I ain't goin' to that place. No
one wants me there, neither," he said,
his eyes fixed on a crushed beer can.
"Now that Londell's outta jail, he got me
workin' so . . . you know how it is."

Harold nodded. He could hear
Grandma's voice in his head. She'd have
told Jupiter to go back to school. He was
about to say it too when a mischievous
smile crept across Jupiter's face.

"Yo, remember that crazy art teacher
we had in sixth grade?"

Harold grinned. "Yeah. Ms. Kowalski.
She used to dye her hair pink."

"Yo, that chick was *crazy*!" said
Jupiter, jumping up from the swing.
"She'd always be wearing sunglasses in
class, talkin' about how we could be anything we wanted. She was cool though.
She used to let me stay after school and
play with all the paints."

"Remember those paper pumpkins

nade for Halloween?" Harold said.

Jupiter nodded, as if he was remembering something wonderful he'd forgotten long ago. "They was cool." Then, Jupiter's smile faded.

"What'chu doin' here, Harold?" he asked. It was the first time in years Harold heard him say his name. "I mean, this don't seem like you," Jupiter continued. "You was always quiet. I remember your grandma, too. She used to come to *everything* at school. Even the stupid stuff."

"She's sick," Harold answered. "We need money. Londell said he could help me out."

Keenan chuckled bitterly and touched his swollen lip. Jupiter spat into the dirt and shook his head slowly.

"What's wrong with your grandma?" he asked after a few moments.

Harold shrugged. "A bunch of stuff."

"My mom's sick too," Jupiter confessed. "Almost died last year."

Harold looked up, surprised. "What happened?" he asked, but Jupiter didn't answer. He was staring off into the distance.

"It ain't fun out here," he finally said, kicking the dusty ground in disgust. "I mean, *look* at this place. What kinda life is this?"

"Londell comin'!" Bug yelled from across the block. His voice shattered the heavy silence of the park.

Harold jumped up from his swing anxiously. *It's about time*, he thought, glancing at his watch. *I gotta get home soon.*

Jupiter lingered for a moment, his eyes focused on the ground as if he was seeing something in the dirt no one else noticed. Then he hurried off to join his brother.

"You Londell's new delivery boy?" Keenan asked once Jupiter was far enough away.

"Yeah," said Harold.

"Be careful, man," Keenan whispered.

"Of what?"

"Of everything," he replied, looking in Londell's direction.

Chapter 7

Londell waved Harold over to the car and handed him two paper bags and a slip of paper.

"Here you go. Two packages, two drops."

Harold recognized the first address; it was the same house he'd gone to yesterday. The second address he didn't know. He shoved the bags into his backpack and stood at the curb waiting.

"Well, what'chu waitin' for?" Londell said impatiently.

"Aren't you gonna drive me?" Harold asked.

"Boy, I ain't your taxi. Yesterday, I was showin' you the ropes. You know what you're doin' now. So go get me my money," he ordered.

"But I gotta be home in two hours," Harold replied, looking at the addresses.

"I don't think I got enough time."

"Fine," Londell snapped. "I'll send Bug instead. I'll give him your money too. Yo Bug!" he shouted.

"No, wait!" Harold cried, glancing at the young boy fiddling with his yellow backpack. Even if he didn't need the money, Harold didn't want Bug out on the streets alone. "I'll do it."

Moments later, Harold was hurrying toward the white house with green shutters. It was ten blocks away, and Harold knew he had to rush to make it home on time. After two blocks, he felt a cramp rip into his stomach. A block further he was gasping for air.

I can't run that far, Harold thought, squatting on the sidewalk to catch his breath. Behind him, the broken front door of a boarded-up house creaked open. Harold took off running again, afraid to look back. He could hear the brown paper bags crunching in his backpack. He felt like a moving target.

Drenched in sweat and out of breath, he finally crossed into the leafy neighborhood Londell had driven through yesterday. An elderly woman with a cart full of groceries passed him on the sidewalk.

"You okay?" she asked. She reminded him of Grandma.

"Yeah," he replied guiltily. His backpack suddenly felt bulky and oversized. *Could she hear the paper bags inside too?* he wondered.

"I'm fine," he said, avoiding her gaze. "I gotta go."

Harold rushed by her then, walking the final two blocks until he reached the white house. The lights were on. Inside he could hear a woman's voice and the clank of dinner plates and silverware.

Harold knocked on the door.

"I'll get it, baby!" he heard a man yell. A few seconds later, Shawn stepped out onto the porch and looked around nervously.

"C'mon, hurry up," he said tensely, scratching at his arm. His face was sickly pale and his eyes looked red and dry.

"It's one hundred dollars," Harold said.

Shawn paused and checked the street. "Where's Londell?" he asked.

Harold didn't like the way he was acting. He seemed tense, more agitated than yesterday.

"He's around the corner," Harold lied.

"Oh," Shawn replied as he reached into his pocket and handed Harold a roll of cash. Remembering Londell's instructions, Harold counted it. There was only sixty dollars.

"It's a hundred," Harold said, trying to sound confident. "You only gave me sixty."

"C'mon kid. Help me out here."

Harold took a step back. "It's one hundred."

"Who's at the door, babe?" the woman called from inside the house.

"No one!" Shawn shouted back. "Wrong house."

"Here," he snapped, shoving forty more dollars into Harold's sweaty hand. "You happy now?"

Harold reached into his backpack.

"Don't come so late next time," Shawn added. "My wife's home now."

Wife? Harold thought. His heart raced as he quickly handed over the paper sack. *What if she comes out here?* Suddenly Harold heard something creeping up the sidewalk close by. He whipped around to see a little girl. She was stopped in front of the house.

"Hi, Mr. Shawn!" she said with a grin.

For an instant, Harold was frozen.

He looked at Shawn, wishing he'd never met him, and then glanced at the little girl. She proudly held out a doll in her small hand.

"It's from Mommy," she chirped, walking toward the house. "Wanna see?"

Harold gasped and lowered his head, unable to look into her eyes. He suddenly felt dirty, unclean. He gripped his backpack, terrified its contents would spill and the child would know why he was there.

"Not now, sweetie!" Shawn called out. He smiled then, a gesture Harold could see took all his effort. "Go home to Mommy!" he said.

"Who's there?" his wife called out from inside the house.

"Get outta here, man!" Shawn whispered angrily to Harold. "*Go!*"

Harold threw his bag over his shoulder and took off down the front walkway. He raced by the little girl, who stumbled backward.

"Mommy!" she hollered.

As Harold passed the house next door, he heard a door creak open and a woman's voice call out. "Maria?! What's wrong, baby?"

Harold pressed his hands to his ears

and ran.

All his life, Grandma had warned him about the guys who dealt drugs and ruined neighborhoods. All his life, she'd fought to keep her block free of drugs and safe for kids to play. And now he'd become the very thing she stood against. His face burned with shame.

He wanted to throw the remaining bag in the gutter and go home. But Londell's warning echoed in his mind: *"Don't you ever come back to me short on what you owe."*

I gotta keep going, he thought, glancing at his watch. *Just one more delivery.*

Harold's heart raced. He tried to push the little girl's face out of his mind, but there it was, condemning him, accusing him, calling him what he was: a drug dealer.

* * *

Harold reached the next address twenty minutes later.

Great, Harold thought, looking up at the dilapidated house. The top two windows were covered in plywood; it was dark, except for a faint light on the first floor. He could see several people moving around inside.

A sick, creeping feeling sank into the pit of Harold's stomach. Every muscle in his body told him to get away, to drop the bag and run, but he knew that wasn't an option.

Just get it over with, he thought.

Harold dragged himself to the front door and knocked. A dog snarled angrily on the other side.

"Who's there?" a voice shouted suspiciously.

Harold wasn't sure what to say. "I'm with Londell," he answered.

The door opened a crack, and a skinny man peered at Harold. "Where's the other boy?" he snarled. "Where's Keenan?"

"He's not here," Harold replied nervously. "I'm Harold."

"You got my stuff?"

"Yeah," said Harold, reaching into his backpack. "It's a hundred dollars."

"Lemme check it first," said the man, looking Harold over.

"The money first," Harold said cautiously.

"How do I know you ain't rippin' me off?" the man replied. "Lemme check the bag."

"I ain't got time for this!" Harold yelled

desperately. "Please, mister. Just gimme the money so I can get outta here!"

The man handed Harold a wad of cash. Harold counted it quickly and shoved the bag into his hands, glad to be rid of it. He hurried back to the playground, which was busier than ever.

Jupiter and Keenan stood together at the far corner, their hands moving swiftly, taking money and giving out what looked like small plastic bags. Harold headed straight for Londell's car, which was parked on a shadowy curb under a broken streetlight.

"Got my money?" Londell asked as Harold climbed into his car.

"Yeah," Harold grumbled, handing him the crumpled, sweaty bills.

"There's my boy!" Londell said approvingly. "And here's your fifty dollars."

Harold grabbed the money, though part of him wanted to leave it right there on the floor of Londell's car.

"That guy I deliver to. He's got a wife," Harold blurted. "And there's a little girl that lives next door."

"*So?*" Londell answered, counting out the cash Harold handed him. "What'd you care?"

"I don't wanna go back there," he

replied. "It's not right."

Londell checked the rearview mirror. "Relax," he said, shifting in his seat. "If he didn't buy from us, he'd buy from someone else."

"She looked right at me," Harold persisted, shaking his head. "I sold her neighbor drugs."

"That's right," Londell replied with a bitter grin. "You're one of us now."

Harold cringed. "I don't wanna go back there," he said again.

Londell's cell phone rang loudly, lighting up the darkness. They both jumped at the sound.

"Yeah?" Londell answered quickly, his voice tense. "Yeah, I'm on my way now. I got your money. Yeah, all of it."

Londell hung up and started the car. "Gotta go. Tell Joop I'll be back later."

Harold swallowed and took a deep breath. "I can't do this anymore, Londell. I'm sorry. I just can't." Harold checked his watch. It was 6:15. He needed to get home.

"What'chu think this is, SuperFoods?" Londell replied with a flash of anger.

"Look, I appreciate all you did, giving me a job and all," Harold continued, putting his hand on the door handle.

"But I can't come back here. Thanks for everything. Really."

Suddenly, Londell grabbed Harold's shirt and yanked him across the car. Harold's head smacked into the console, and then he heard something click. Before he could react, he felt a stabbing pain under his chin. Londell was leaning over him, holding a switchblade at his throat.

"Where you think you're going?" Londell growled. "You owe me, boy. Didn't I help you when you didn't have no money? Didn't I give you a job when you came looking for it? You belong to me now. There ain't no quittin'."

The blade bit into the soft flesh of Harold's chin. Londell's eyes blazed with rage.

"Please!" Harold cried. He tried to pull away, but Londell only tightened his grip. "I'll pay you back!"

The rearview mirror suddenly lit up with the headlights of an approaching car. Londell ducked, shoving Harold's head lower.

"Git down!" he whispered nervously, holding the knife at Harold's neck. The car passed and Londell looked up.

"I ain't goin' back to jail," he insisted,

staring at the red taillights fading in the distance. "And you ain't quittin', understand? I know where you live. I know where you go to school. I know you ain't got no daddy to run home to. I even know about your poor sick grandma. You better keep your mouth shut. And you better be here Monday," he warned.

"Londell, please," Harold pleaded. "I won't say nothing, I swear. I won't tell anybody!"

"Oh I know you won't," Londell growled, pushing the knife tightly against his skin.

"Okay!" Harold gasped. "Please, just let me go. I'll come back Monday! I swear!"

Londell relaxed his grip, and Harold pulled himself free.

"You had a good day, Harold. You made your drops and came back with my money. Don't get soft on me now. You just getting started."

Harold opened the door and tumbled onto the sidewalk.

"What's goin' on?" Jupiter called from the corner.

"Mind your business!" Londell shouted back.

Harold staggered to his feet and

rubbed his chin. A bead of blood coated his finger. For a moment, his eyes locked with Keenan's and Jupiter's. He could see fear on their faces as they slowly walked toward the car. He knew at that moment how Keenan injured his lip and how Jupiter's face got bruised: Londell. The truth crashed through his mind like a gunshot.

Londell lied. He doesn't care about us. All he wants is money. And I got no way out.

Harold turned away and bolted down the street, his heart pounding so hard he could feel it throb in his throat. He made it halfway to the bus stop before his stomach heaved. He doubled over and threw up, the mess of his sandwich splattering at his feet.

What am I gonna do? he thought desperately, burying his head in his hands.

"Yo Harold, you okay?" Harold looked up to see Bug running toward him.

"Bug!" he cried, wiping his mouth on his T-shirt. "Listen to me. You gotta get outta here. Understand? Go home, and don't ever come back here. No matter what Londell says."

"What'chu talkin' about? Why you throwin' up in the street?" Bug reached out and pointed to Harold's chin. "You bleedin', Harold!" he cried.

"It's okay. I'm all right." Harold replied, searching his backpack until he found a notebook and pen. "Listen to me. Here's my address and phone number. You keep this with you. If you ever need me, you find me, okay?"

"Okay," the boy agreed, studying Harold.

"I'm serious, Bug. Londell don't care about y—" Harold stopped himself. He wanted to protect Bug, not frighten him. "Just don't come back here no more. Take the money Londell paid you and don't come back."

"Londell got my money. He say I'm too young, so he holdin' it for me. He do give me food, though," Bug said innocently.

Harold rolled his eyes in disgust. "Tell you what," he said, trying to sound calm. "I'll give you all the sandwiches you want if you promise me you won't come back here, okay?"

"But Londell say—"

"I know what he says!" Harold interrupted. "But sometimes grown-ups don't tell the truth. Do you trust me, Bug?"

"Yeah," he said, nodding his head.

"You nice."

"Good. Then you gotta listen to me, okay?"

"Okay," Bug agreed.

"You gotta go home," Harold said. "Go home to your foster mom. Run! You hear me? *Run!*"

Bug took off down the block and Harold watched as his yellow backpack disappeared out of sight. Then Harold ran to the bus stop, wiping his chin with his T-shirt.

He pays him in cheeseburgers, Harold thought angrily. *He told me he looked after Bug, but he's using him. Just like me.*

Harold paced the sidewalk, watching for the headlights of the bus, praying he'd make it home in one piece.

What've I done? he thought desperately. *What've I done?*

Chapter 8

Forty-five minutes later, Harold staggered into his apartment building. The bus was late, and he knew Grandma would be angry.

What am I gonna tell her? he thought, making sure there was no blood on his chin. *I'm running out of excuses.*

He walked down the hall and noticed his apartment door was open. Then he heard someone crying. Harold dropped his backpack and ran inside.

"*Grandma?!*" he yelled. She was lying on the kitchen floor, clutching her leg and shivering. Her crutches were strewn next to her, and blood trickled from her wound, soaking the white bandage. Cindy was kneeling beside her. Tears streamed down her frightened face.

"Harold!" Cindy cried. "She fell! I heard her yelling from my apartment!"

Harold dropped to the floor. "Don't move, Grandma. It's okay. I'm here."

"Where were you?" Cindy whispered, shooting him an accusatory look. "She was calling for you."

"Oh, Grandma . . . I'm so sorry," he wailed.

"I'm okay," Grandma said slowly, pressing her hand to her forehead. Her eyes were slightly glazed, and she slurred her words. "I needed something to eat . . . must've slipped. I don't remember."

"Should we call an ambulance?" Cindy asked. He could hear the terror in her voice.

"I don't know!" Harold cried, staring helplessly at Grandma's pained face. He tried to remember what the doctors at the hospital told him, but his mind was a blur of panic. "I don't know what to do!"

This is all my fault! he thought. *I was supposed to be here!* Harold raced down the hallway and banged on Mr. Harris's door.

"Please!" he pleaded. "Please be home!"

"What's wrong?" Mr. Harris said as he opened the door.

"Grandma fell!" Harold yelled. "She's on the floor!"

Mr. Harris ran to Harold's apartment and crouched beside Grandma. "Can you move?" he asked softly, touching her leg.

"I think so," she answered. "I'm a little dizzy."

"Harold, get me some juice from the fridge," Mr. Harris commanded, his voice calm and focused. "Cindy, bring me a pillow and blanket."

Cindy rushed to Grandma's room and returned with her pillow and comforter. Harold's hands were shaking uncontrollably. He grabbed a glass and filled it with orange juice, spilling much of it on the counter.

"Here!" he said, handing it to Mr. Harris. "Should I call an ambulance?"

"I don't think we need to," he replied as he propped up her head with a pillow and covered her with the blanket. "Go into the living room with Cindy and wait there. She's gonna be okay. She just needs to get her blood sugar up. My aunt was the same way. C'mon, Mrs. Rose. You need to drink some juice."

Harold and Cindy paced in the living room while Mr. Harris calmly talked to Grandma.

"Where were you?" Cindy whispered, her voice a mixture of anger and worry.

"What happened to your chin?"

"It's nothing," he replied. There was no way he could tell her the truth. "I fell."

"Harold, I need your help," Mr. Harris said after a few moments.

Grandma seemed more alert, and Mr. Harris gently sat her up. "Now just put your arms around my neck," he said as he crouched in front of her, locking his arms around her waist. "On the count of three now," he continued, hoisting her up off the floor.

Harold picked up her crutches and together they led her carefully to her bedroom. Then Mr. Harris had Harold bring her a plate of sliced apples and cheese, which she ate hungrily, while he cleaned and changed her bandage.

"I'm so sorry," Harold said, guilt stabbing at his chest. "I'll never be late again. I swear it."

"We'll talk about it tomorrow," she said in a sad voice. "I need to rest now."

Harold was furious at himself for talking to Londell, for ever thinking he could trust him.

All I wanted to do was help. Instead, I've made things worse, he thought as he turned off the light and gently closed her bedroom door. And yet there was no way to escape Londell. He'd be waiting again Monday with more drugs to sell. Harold's head pounded with stress.

"She'll be fine," assured Mr. Harris as Harold stepped into the hallway. "I'll be by tomorrow to check on her, and to take you to the grocery store."

"Thanks," Harold said, his mind spinning. "Sorry. For bothering you, I mean."

"It's not a bother," he replied. "I'm just up the hall if you need me."

Harold changed his T-shirt and went back into the living room. Cindy was sitting on the couch. He could tell she was waiting for him.

"Is she gonna be okay?" Cindy asked.

Harold plopped down wearily next to her. "Yeah. I think so." He said, unable to look into her eyes. "Thanks for coming over and for those bandages. I'm sorry, Cindy . . . sorry about everything."

"Harold, what happened to you?" she said. He could feel her staring at him.

"Nothin'," he said, leaning back and folding his arms over his head the way he did when he had a bad headache. Anything to hide his face. "The bus back from 25th Street was running late, that's all."

"*25th Street!* Is that where you were? Is that where you got that cut?"

Harold shrugged. He didn't want to lie, but the truth was so ugly he couldn't speak it. And then there was Londell's warning not to talk. Harold knew Cindy was safer if she didn't know anything.

"So it's gonna be like *that*? You're not even going to talk to me after all this?" Cindy asked, her voice rising in frustration. "You know, Harold, I don't even know who you are anymore. I mean, I used to think I could trust you with anything. You were the only guy I could say that about." She paused, sighing as if what she had said hurt her. Then she got up and walked toward the door. "But now you're different. You changed since you started talking to Londell. I don't even know what to think now."

He wanted to reach out to her, tell her the truth about everything, and ask her not to leave him alone in the living room. But the words stuck in his throat. Instead, he forced himself to look at her face and stare into her piercing amber eyes.

"I'm still the same, Cindy," he managed to say. "Remember that, no matter what happens. I didn't change."

* * *

Saturday morning, Grandma was unusually quiet. Harold had expected her to yell at him for being so late last night, but she didn't. Instead she kept watching him, a concerned look on her face.

"What happened to your chin?" she asked over breakfast.

"Nothing," he replied. "I fell. At work."

Grandma looked at him skeptically. "You know you can talk to me, child. If something's wrong, if you're in some sort of trouble . . ."

"I'm fine," he replied quickly. "Really."

"Harold, I know these past few weeks have been hard on you," she continued, looking up at the faded photograph of her husband. "I know I haven't been myself, with all this nonsense with my leg and my diabetes. But things'll get better, baby. I'm feeling stronger every day. In a few weeks, I'll start my physical therapy and I'll get back on my feet. And I'll make sure I test my blood from now on."

Grandma reached across the table and grabbed Harold's hand. "We're gonna be okay," she insisted in a strong, clear voice.

Harold forced himself to smile. "I know," he lied, touching the painful cut on his chin.

* * *

Later that afternoon, Harold headed to SuperFoods with Mr. Harris.

Harold was glad it was the weekend when Mr. Marshall was off as they made their way through the produce aisle, filling their cart with fruits and vegetables. Harold tried to listen as Mr. Harris explained which foods were best for Grandma, but his mind kept wandering.

Whenever he closed his eyes, he saw Grandma lying helpless on the cold kitchen floor, little Maria staring at him with her accusing eyes, Londell's knife flashing in the darkness. They were nightmare images Harold couldn't escape, even with Mr. Harris at his side.

"You okay?" Mr. Harris asked as they unloaded their groceries at the checkout counter. "You're awful quiet today."

Harold nodded sadly. "Just tired, I guess."

He liked Mr. Harris a lot. The man made him feel safer, just by being nearby. But he also made him sad inside. No matter how helpful Mr. Harris was, he was just their neighbor. He couldn't solve their problems. He'd move away at some point, Harold figured. Then he and Grandma would be alone again.

Harold remembered the Family Services letter and shuddered. It was just a matter of time before Grandma wouldn't be able to care for him. *And then what?* Harold wondered.

"You wanna shoot some hoops after we're done here?" Mr. Harris suggested, snapping Harold from his thoughts as they left SuperFoods.

"Okay," Harold replied, stopping dead in his tracks.

A familiar gold Nissan was parked at the curb in front of them. Londell was sitting in the driver's seat. He stared right at them, his mouth curled into a sneer.

Oh God! Harold thought, looking nervously at Mr. Harris. He wanted to run back into the store, but he couldn't move.

Mr. Harris seemed to know something was wrong. He glanced at Harold, then at Londell.

"Who's that, Harold?" he asked, his voice suddenly serious.

Harold shook his head, unable to speak. His eyes locked with Londell's.

"Harold, look at me," Mr. Harris persisted. "Who is that?"

Again, Harold said nothing.

Then Mr. Harris put down the groceries and walked over to the car.

What's he doing? Harold thought with a flash of panic. *Londell's gonna kill him!*

"Something I can help you with?" Mr. Harris boomed, staring Londell dead in the eye.

Londell looked at him suspiciously.

"You like staring down kids?" Mr. Harris challenged.

"Mind your business, old man," he hissed.

Mr. Harris didn't budge. He stood there, blocking Londell's view of Harold, his legs slightly apart, his back straight, his shoulders perfectly squared. To Harold he was like a superhero, unmovable, powerful, unafraid.

"This *is* my business, *young* man," said Mr. Harris. "This is my neighborhood and Harold's with me. So I'm right where I should be."

Mr. Harris leaned in close to Londell, who shifted in his seat. "Now I suggest

117

you get movin' and take that stare of yours somewhere else."

Londell smirked as if Mr. Harris had said something amusing. But Harold could see a flash of surprise in Londell's dark eyes. Maybe even a touch of fear.

Just then Jupiter sprinted around the corner. He stopped when he saw the two men facing off. A brown paper bag peeked out from the waist of his baggy jeans. He glanced back at Harold and then at Mr. Harris.

"What's goin' on?" he said.

"Get in the car, Joop," Londell snapped.

Mr. Harris stepped back, giving Jupiter just enough room to climb in next to his brother. Then Londell rolled up the window and pulled away from the curb. As the car passed, Jupiter's eyes met Harold's. He looked worried, like he wished he could stay behind.

"C'mon. Let's go," said Mr. Harris, putting his arm protectively around Harold's shoulders.

That was awesome! Harold thought with a smile. He knew Londell would be furious, but for the moment, Harold didn't care. Mr. Harris had stared Londell down. Harold still couldn't believe it.

"You be careful of that one," Mr. Harris warned. "He's got some fire in him. And who was that other boy?"

"His younger brother," Harold said.

Mr. Harris shook his head with anger. "I swear, this neighborhood hasn't changed since I was your age."

"You grew up around here?" Harold asked.

Mr. Harris nodded. "Three blocks from here. This place was crawling with dealers back then, too."

"How'd you know he's a dealer?"

"Am I wrong?" Mr. Harris replied knowingly.

"No," Harold admitted, grateful Mr. Harris didn't ask him any questions about Londell.

Chapter 9

Monday afternoon, Harold waited for Cindy at her locker. Unable to sleep the night before, he'd imagined this moment for hours, but his stomach still trembled when their eyes met.

"Cindy, I meant what I said to you the other day," he said, handing her money for the bandages she'd bought for Grandma. "It's still me. I haven't changed at all."

"Harold, where'd you get this money?"

"Please, Cindy, just take it. It's yours."

"Whatever you're doing, Harold, you need to stop," Cindy demanded, dropping the money as if it burned her fingers.

"I can't, Cindy!" he snapped. "It's too late for that now. You were right about Londell, but I needed money to help Grandma. It was stupid, I know. But there's no walkin' away. I'm trapped."

"Harold, you gotta tell someone

before you get hurt," she urged, touching his arm. "I'll go with you. Maybe we can tell the police or Mr. Mitchell—"

"Listen, I know you want to help, but you gotta stay out of this. This is *my* problem," he said, adjusting his backpack.

"Harold—"

"I'm sorry, Cindy. But I gotta go," he said, forcing himself to walk away before he allowed his problems to swallow her, too.

"*Harold!*" she called.

* * *

Forty-five minutes later, Harold stepped off the bus and headed toward the abandoned playground. Dark, angry clouds gathered in the gray sky overhead, making the streets seem more desolate than ever. Harold pulled his jacket tightly around himself and walked up the block, glass crunching under his feet as he passed beneath the broken streetlights.

Londell's car was parked at the playground. Jupiter and Keenan stood nearby. Harold was relieved that Bug wasn't there. *At least he's safe*, Harold thought. *At least one of us is safe.*

Jupiter and Keenan backed away as

Harold approached the car, as if he had a disease they didn't want to catch.

"Get over here," Londell growled, grabbing Harold by the collar through the driver's window. "Who was that man yesterday? Actin' like he was your daddy."

"He's nobody," Harold murmured. "He's just a neighbor."

"He's lucky I didn't shoot him right there in the street. You better keep your mouth shut, boy. 'Cause he can't save you. Nobody can."

I know, he thought miserably.

Londell pushed Harold away in disgust. Then he handed him three paper bags and a slip of paper. "Get going, boy. You got a long night ahead of you."

Three? Harold thought. *I'll never make it home in time!* He knew there was no point in arguing; Londell didn't care about his problems.

Harold shoved the bags into his backpack and headed in the direction of the first address: Shawn's house.

Please don't let little Maria be there, he prayed.

Harold passed by Jupiter, who was rubbing the scar on his hand and staring at the ground. Harold thought he looked ashamed.

Twenty minutes later, Harold stood on Shawn's clean porch. Large drops of rain pattered on the sidewalk as he raised his hand to knock on the door. Twice he stopped himself, checking the street, making sure Maria was inside.

This is wrong, he kept thinking as his stomach churned. *I don't want to do this.*

Suddenly the door opened. Shawn stepped outside, pale-faced, barefooted, and extremely anxious. His button-down shirt was hanging out of his pants. Inside the house, the television blared loudly. There were no sounds of dinner being cooked. The car was missing from the driveway.

"You're late," he barked. "Gimme my stuff."

Harold sighed and reached into his backpack. "It's a hundred bucks," he said.

"Where's Londell?" Shawn asked, glancing down the block.

"He's not here," Harold answered, pulling out the bag.

"Tell him I'll pay him tomorrow," said Shawn, his fingers twitching at the sight of the paper bag. Harold took a step back.

"C'mon, kid. Londell knows me. He'll understand."

"I need you to pay me *now*," Harold insisted.

Suddenly Shawn lunged forward, slamming his fist into the side of Harold's forehead. Harold stumbled backward, stunned. For a moment, everything went dark and his ears rang loudly from the punch.

"What're you doing, man?!" Harold exclaimed, shaking his head. Shawn lunged again, swinging wildly. Harold ducked, avoiding the blow, but the man kept coming like an enraged animal.

Crunch!

Shawn's fist landed squarely on Harold's nose. Blood gushed instantly, spilling down his face and onto his shirt, dripping like thick red paint on the white porch.

"Gimme it!" Shawn growled, groping for the bag in Harold's hands.

He's gonna kill me! Harold thought. He could taste something salty spilling down the back of his throat, filling his mouth. Harold coughed and spat a wet clot of blood.

"Take it!" Harold shouted, dropping the bag and holding up his hands to protect his face. "Just lemme go!" His voice gurgled and he coughed again, spewing more blood.

Shawn fell to his knees and ripped the bag open, revealing several small glass vials filled with what looked like white powder.

For a moment, Harold was frozen, shocked from the pain in his head and the sight of a grown man kneeling on a bloody porch clutching a bag of what Harold knew was poison. Pure poison.

Then Harold snapped.

With a burst of adrenaline, he took off running, down the front steps and onto the street. He ran through the rain like his life depended on it, his panicked heart hammering in his chest. His crushed nose throbbed, and tears streamed from his eyes, mixing with rain and blood and sweat. His legs burned and shook, but he kept on running, as fast as he could, for as long as he could. The world passed by in a blur of cars, houses, people, traffic lights, corners and stores, until he finally arrived at the only place he could think of going, the only place he truly wanted to be, despite everything: Home.

Harold burst into his apartment, dropping his backpack on the floor, and headed straight into the bathroom, locking the door behind him.

"Harold!" Grandma shrieked, but he didn't answer. He stared aghast at the bathroom mirror. A ruined version of himself gazed back. His nose was purple and swollen. Dark blood had caked beneath his nostrils, covering his chin and staining his T-shirt. A painful lump was forming on the side of his forehead.

What am I gonna do?! he thought.

"Harold!" Grandma shrieked again, banging on the door. "You get out here this instant!"

"Just gimme a minute!" he shouted back.

Harold peeled off his clothes, turned on the shower and climbed into the bathtub, letting the hot water stream down his face. A pink pool sloshed over his feet.

How am I gonna explain this? What am I gonna do about Londell?

Harold stood in the shower until his shaking fingers wrinkled like raisins and there was no hot water left. Then he climbed out, put on his filthy clothes, and walked into the kitchen.

Grandma was standing at the sink, leaning on her crutches. His backpack lay open on the table. Two paper bags sat on the counter.

"Grandma, no!" he screamed. In her hands were several glass vials. The fine white powder poured down the drain.

"Sit down!" she boomed. "You sit down, Harold, and don't you say a word to me!" She was furious.

"Is this what you've been up to?" she hollered. "Drugs, Harold? *Drugs?* My God, child. I knew something was going on with you, but *this?*" she yelled, shaking an empty vial at him. "In *my* house?!"

"I'm sorry, Grandma!"

"*Sorry?!*" Grandma shouted. "Look at you! Is this what you want to be? Is this how I raised you? I called SuperFoods today. You quit last week! You've been lying to me all this time so you could sell *this?!*" She slammed the vial down into the sink with a loud thud. "Shame on you, child!"

"I was trying to help. I swear, Grandma."

"Don't you dare say that to me," she fumed. "Ain't no help comes from this poison!"

"But I saw the hospital bills! I know how much we owe! I know about everything!"

Grandma stepped back as if his

words hurt her. Then her eyes widened.

"What are you talking about, child?"

"I read the letter! I know I have no guardian! And if you can't afford to keep me—"

"Harold, what are you saying?" Grandma whispered, her voice softening. "My God, child. Is that was this is about?"

Suddenly, Harold thought about Londell. He looked at the clock. It was 6:30. Londell would be waiting for him. And now, Harold didn't have the money or the drugs.

I know where you live. I know where you go to school. I know you ain't got no daddy to run home to. Londell's words growled in his head.

He's gonna come for me. And if he comes here . . .

Harold looked at Grandma and the empty bags on the counter.

I gotta protect her, he thought.

Harold turned and raced to the door.

"Where are you going? You sit down, Harold!" she yelled, turning on her crutches.

"I can't," he groaned. "I'm sorry, Grandma. You don't understand. I gotta go."

Before she could react, Harold opened

the door and took off down the hall.

"Harold!" she screamed. He heard a door click open as he rushed past, but he didn't stop.

I gotta go back to the playground, he thought. *If I don't, Londell's gonna come here.*

* * *

It was dark and pouring when Harold reached the bus stop. Moments later, the bus appeared, and he dragged himself aboard. He knew he looked terrible. He caught the bus driver staring at his blood-splattered shirt. A woman in the front row glared at him and clutched her pocketbook as he walked by. He kept his head down and moved quickly to the nearest seat.

Harold's knees shook uncontrollably as the bus lumbered forward. He had no idea what Londell would do to him, but he had to go to the playground. Otherwise, Londell would come to the apartment for him, and someone else could get hurt Maybe Grandma or Cindy.

How did I get here? he thought. *Why did I ever trust Londell?* Tears swelled in his eyes as he thought about Grandma teetering on her crutches, her hands covered in white dust. He'd never seen her so angry.

I've lost everything, Harold sobbed. *Grandma will never forgive me. Neither will Cindy. And now I gotta face Londell. Alone.*

Harold got off at 25th Street and headed toward the playground. He could see the red brake lights of Londell's car, like angry red eyes in the darkness. Keenan hurried toward him. He looked worried.

"Londell's waitin' for you," he said urgently, glancing at Harold's swollen face and filthy shirt. "What *happened*, man?"

"You should get outta here," Harold said. "Go home, Kee."

"You know I can't leave. Londell will kill me."

You and me both, Harold thought as he kept walking, forcing himself forward.

"You're late," Londell barked as Harold approached the car. "Looks like you had a rough night," he added with a laugh. Jupiter sat beside his brother; his eyes locked with Harold's. "I ain't got all night," Londell continued, holding out his hand.

Harold took a deep breath. "I don't have your money," he said. "I don't have your drugs either."

"What'd you say?" Londell growled, stepping out of the car. His dark eyes flashed with rage.

Harold stumbled backward into the street, raising his hands to protect himself. "I don't have your money, Londell. It wasn't my fault. That dude Shawn, he attacked me. He took the bag."

Londell was starting to look nervous. "What about the other two bags?" he asked.

"They're gone," Harold answered, his voice cracking. He couldn't mention Grandma.

"What'd you mean, *gone*?" Londell said anxiously.

Jupiter jumped out of the car. "C'mon bro, chill out," he pleaded. "You know how these junkies be. It ain't his fault."

"Shut up, Joop," Londell spat, storming up to Harold.

"Londell, please," Harold cried. "I'll pay you back! I'll figure something out, I swear!"

"There ain't no paying back," he snarled. "I need that money now!" Before Harold knew what was happening, Londell grabbed him by the throat and whipped him around, slamming him up against the car. Harold gasped as Londell's grip tightened around his throat.

"Please!" he wheezed. "Don't hurt me, man!"

"Get over here, Joop. Help me hold this fat boy down," Londell snarled.

"Bro, c'mon!" Jupiter cried. "Just let him go. I'll cover for him this time. You know I been savin'."

Londell released Harold, who collapsed into the street, grasping his neck. He tried to get up, but Londell shoved his white sneaker into Harold's chest, pinning him to the ground.

"Come here, Joop. Teach this boy a lesson."

Harold's body was trembling. "Please!" he cried, covering his head. "I'll do anything you want!"

"Shut your mouth, boy! Joop, get over here. *Now!*"

Joop shook his head and backed away, his eyes wild with fear. "Londell, c'mon man! I don't wanna hit him!"

"Do it!" Londell ordered.

Chapter 10

Screech!

Suddenly a car skidded to a stop behind them. Harold heard a door open and the quick thud of steps. Then a man's scream pierced the darkness.

Harold scampered to his feet and turned back to see Mr. Harris land a crushing punch into Londell's cheek. His head snapped back with the blow, and he sank to the asphalt. Londell tried to stand, reaching for something in his belt, but Mr. Harris hit him again. His fist struck like a hammer into Londell's jaw.

Londell sprawled forward, and a small black handgun slipped from his fingers and slid just a few feet from where Harold and Jupiter were standing. Londell stretched for it, but Mr. Harris grabbed his arm, twisting it up behind his back so he couldn't move.

"Joop!" Londell roared, trying to escape. "Get the gun!"

Jupiter stared at the gun and then at Harold and his brother. Keenan stood in the shadows nearby, his mouth open in disbelief.

"Get it!" Londell barked.

"Don't listen to him, son." Mr. Harris said firmly. "That's not an answer for you. Your brother's made his choice, but you don't have to go down that road."

"Joop! He ain't a cop. Get the gun. Do what you gotta do!" Londell boomed, trying to free himself. Mr. Harris yanked his arm, and Londell shrieked in pain.

Jupiter flinched at the sound, stepping forward slightly. His face was twisted in agony, his eyes on the gun. Harold saw his hand reach out then, the jagged line of his scar faintly visible in the darkness.

A police siren wailed in the distance.

"Don't do it, Joop," Harold said, moving in front of Jupiter, blocking his path. "It don't have to be this way. We used to be in school together, bro. We still can be."

"Get the gun!"

Jupiter stared into Harold's face, studied his bloodied nose and swollen eyes. He shook his head sadly. "It's all wrong. It ain't supposed to be like this. He's my brother."

134

"Shoot him!" Londell struggled to break Mr. Harris's grip. The siren grew louder.

"Go home, Joop," Mr. Harris said, pinning Londell against his car. "Working out here is a game you can't win. You'll end up dead before you're twenty-five. I've seen too much of that. Just walk away while you still can."

"*Shoot him!*"

"C'mon, Joop," Keenan urged. "Let's get outta here."

Jupiter sighed and glanced at Harold. His eyes were swollen and teary, a look that reminded Harold of years earlier when they were just two boys on the school playground.

"I'll take care of Momma," Jupiter said to Londell. And then he turned and disappeared into the darkness with Keenan.

Londell slumped to his knees in defeat as two police cars raced into the park toward them.

* * *

An hour later, for the second time in his life, Harold drove home with Mr. Harris.

"The police are gonna need a statement

from you," he explained. "I'll take you down to the station once you get cleaned up."

"What's gonna happen?" Harold asked.

"Londell's gonna do hard time," Mr. Harris replied gravely. "The police said they've been building a case against him for a drive-by shooting last year. And now he's got drugs and weapons charges. Barely twenty years old, and he's looking at years behind bars. It's sad, but it could have been a lot worse," Mr. Harris added, looking at Harold.

"How did you *find* me?" Harold asked.

"You can thank Cindy for that. She told us where you were. Your grandma called the police right away, but I wasn't going to wait for them," Mr. Harris said, shaking his head. "Glad I didn't."

"I-I don't know how to thank you," Harold stammered. "You could've been killed."

"It's fine, Harold," he said with a deep sigh. "I've risked my life for much less."

At home, Harold opened the door to see Grandma and Cindy sitting on the edge of the couch, their hands clasped tightly together. In the kitchen was the stack of bills Harold had read. The letter from Family Services was there too. Harold could see that Grandma had been looking at them.

"Oh my goodness, Harold!" Cindy cried, glancing at his nose and then hugging him. "Are you okay?"

"Yeah," he answered softly, putting his arm around her for the first time.

"Come over here, Harold," Grandma snapped.

Harold stepped away from Cindy and sat next to Grandma, hanging his head in shame. "I'm so sorry," he whispered, preparing to hear her yell at him. *I deserve it,* he thought. *I deserve whatever punishment she gives me.*

Grandma grabbed him and pressed his head to her shoulder, holding him so tightly he could barely breathe.

"Oh my child, my child," she repeated, rocking him like she did when he was a young boy. "Don't you know how much I love you? I would give my life for you, child. I would give my life before I let someone take you away from me."

Harold's eyes filled with tears. "You're not mad?" he asked softly, lifting his head.

"Of course I'm mad!" she said sternly. "You could've gotten yourself killed!" Then her voice became tender. "But I didn't realize how frightened you've been these past few weeks. Worrying about money, and that damn letter from Family Services."

"What letter?" Mr. Harris asked.

"On the table," she replied with a sigh. "Harold, those hospital bills, most of them are covered by our insurance. And whatever's left, I'll manage to pay it off over time."

"But you said we had no money!" Harold cried. "You said—"

"I *said* you should let *me* worry about how we're gonna pay the bills! Why didn't you talk to me about this? Yes, money's tight right now, but we'll be fine. We'll be just fine. Haven't I always taken care of you?"

"What about the letter? If something happens to you, they're gonna take me away!"

Grandma sighed. "Nothing's gonna happen to me, Harold. I'm okay. No one's gonna take you anywhere."

"But you're sick!" he cried, jumping up from the couch. "What if you go back to the hospital? What if you get worse?"

Mr. Harris stood in front of the kitchen table, listening carefully. A look of concern spread across his face as he read over the letter.

Grandma sighed. "I don't know," she admitted, her eyes moist. "I suppose I've been avoiding this conversation."

"He could stay with me!" Cindy offered.

"It doesn't work that way, sweetie." Grandma declared.

Suddenly, Mr. Harris marched across the room and grabbed a pen from their coffee table. Then he walked back into the kitchen and without saying a word, he signed the form.

"Markus, stop it," Grandma yelled. "I can't ask you to do that. You've done enough for this family. More than it was fair of us to ask."

"Mrs. Rose," he said calmly, "I came back to this neighborhood for a reason. I grew up here without a father, just like Harold. I've had my struggles too. You're gonna be fine, and Harold doesn't need to worry about losing you for a long, long time. But if putting my name on that form will ease his fears, if I can offer him a little comfort, then that's fine by me."

Cindy jumped up and threw her arms around Mr. Harris's waist.

"Okay, okay," he said, patting her head.

Harold was stunned. With one move of the pen, Mr. Harris had changed his world forever. It was a miracle.

"I-I don't know what to say," Harold stammered, his eyes welling up.

"Just learn from this Harold," he replied, opening the door to leave. "You're worth fighting for, son. Don't you ever forget that."

Mr. Harris's words nearly knocked Harold over. The events of the past few weeks had filled him with shame and made him hate what he'd become. And yet, despite his mistakes, there were people still there for him. Together they had pulled him back from a sea of trouble and rescued him when he thought it was impossible. He owed each of them a debt he wasn't sure he could repay. But he would try. Harold was sure of that.

The invisible chains that held him were suddenly broken. And for the first time he could remember, his spirit soared free.